ANGELINA

TERESA GABELMAN

CHAPTER 1

*A*ngelina sat at a table inside the small coffee shop. She hadn't seen her mother for well over a month because her stepfather had been home. They only met when her stepfather was out on the road for his job as a truck driver. Glancing at her phone she frowned. Her mother was never on time. She used to worry about it, but finally realized that was just the way her mom was.

Taking a drink of her coffee she looked out the window ignoring the other customers who were quietly talking at their own tables. It was hard for her to see others enjoying time together. She knew that was selfish on her part, but she couldn't help it. Her life was in such disarray that almost anything made her sad. It sucked. She hated it. Angelina was working through her issues, but some days it was harder than others and today was one of her bad days.

It had been three weeks since she had walked away from her life with Adam. She missed him so damn much it practically tore her apart. He texted her every night to make sure she was okay, asked if she needed anything and she would only reply that she was fine. That was it, nothing more. She made herself turn off her phone after that afraid she would cave and beg him for forgiveness. Anger burned deep inside her. Why in the hell hadn't he done that before she walked out of his life. Why do it now? Dammit and damn him. Was it enough? No, it wasn't, but it was something.

"No." She whispered to herself, even shook her head. It was not enough, and she deserved more. She repeated that thought in her head over and over again.

"Sorry I'm late." Her mother's voice snapped her out of her thoughts.

Angelina looked at her mother who scooted into the booth. She looked thinner than the last time she had seen her. Her hair was dyed an inky black making her already pale complexion ghostly. "You dyed your hair." Angelina observed out loud.

Her hand went to her hair self-consciously after she sat her bag on the table. "Dan prefers brunettes."

Angelina rolled her eyes at that with a snort. Her mother had beautiful blonde hair with light streaks of grey when not colored. Maggie Adams had been a beautiful woman. You could still see her beauty at times, but the hard life she had lived showed through more often than not. She also noticed the huge black sunglasses her mother was wearing and knew the reason. It was an overcast November day, no sun in sight, and being inside her mother didn't even attempt to remove the sunglasses that were way too big for her face.

"Do you like it?" Her mother asked after ordering a coffee from the waitress.

"It's okay, but I like your natural color." Angelina replied honestly, then added with a frown. "How bad was it this time?"

Maggie frowned shifting uncomfortably. "How bad was what?"

"You are wearing sunglasses on a cloudy day inside a restaurant." Angelina said hating having this conversation which seemed to be a repeat from many conversations she'd had with her mother.

Angelina knew her mother's habits so well. For instance, she was fidgeting with the napkin and tearing little pieces off with one hand which was a clear indication she was agitated. Angelina also knew that even behind the sunglasses her mother's eyes were not meeting hers.

"Can't we ever have a normal mother/daughter conversation Angelina?" Her mother whispered with a hiss.

"Nothing about us has ever been normal, mom." Angelina replied trying her best not to feel bad. Maggie Adams had the worst tastes in men and Dan wasn't even the worst of the bunch. Sad, but true. She loved her mother because...well, she was her mother, but there had been, and she was afraid would always be, an anger toward her that would never go away. "What was it this time, mom? Not enough salt in his food? His clothes weren't washed and folded the way he wanted them to be? His beer wasn't cold enough for him?"

"Do you enjoy this?" Her mother tilted her head now looking at her through those dark sunglasses. "Do you enjoy making me feel like a total piece of shit?"

"You aren't the piece of shit, mom." Angelina sighed rubbing her tired eyes. "You just attract pieces of shit."

"Dan loves me, Angelina." Her mother said as if trying to convince her. "You don't see us together when things are good."

Angelina knew she would never get through to her mother, and yet she tried. Dan was an asshole who treated her mother like dirt. He had treated her even worse, almost like a slave and yet her mother always took up for him with some excuse or another.

"Things have gotten better since you moved out." Her mother continued then gasped when she realized what she said. "I'm sorry. It's just Dan had a hard time because you weren't his. You know…"

To say her mother picking a controlling abuser over her didn't hurt would be a lie, but that had been her life growing up. Not anymore. She did what she could for her mother, but unfortunately it was her mother's life to live as she saw fit. There was nothing Angelina could do.

"Yeah, I know." Angelina sighed, then took a drink of her coffee wishing she had waited a little while longer when she was better mentally to see her mother.

"And things have been pretty good. I got a decent job that Dan approves of. He is really proud of me." Her mother smiled, then winced as if in pain. Angelina knew it was from the black eye behind the glasses.

"Oh, he is? So, what was this?" Angelina motioned toward the glasses. "His goodbye gift to you? Something to remember him by while he's out on the road?" She knew she was being a bitch and her mother didn't deserve it, but dammit seeing her mother like this and taking it as if it was normal made her crazy.

"If this is the way you are going to be I'm leaving." Her mother grabbed her bag and started to scoot out of the booth. "I was excited to see you, but I don't want my own daughter treating me this way."

Angelina sighed grabbing her mother's arm. "I'm sorry." She said, hating herself and yet felt some things needed to be said in hopes that maybe just maybe one little thing would click in her mother's mind that Angelina was right. She deserved better. "I just worry about you, mom."

"Well don't." Her mother said as she put her bag back down. "I'm fine. And honestly, this is the first time in a very long time Dan has hit me. Ever since your young man threatened him, Dan has been...better."

The mention of Adam had Angelina's heart twisting and her stomach churning. "That's good." Was all she could manage to say.

"How is Adam?" Her mother asked as the waitress brought her mother's coffee. "I saw him on television during the football game. I hope you got to go and support him, Angelina. You know you never missed one of his football games."

"He's fine. And yes, I went for a few minutes." Angelina replied, then cleared her throat wanting nothing more than to change the subject. She hadn't told her that she had left Adam. She had, in fact, gone to support Adam during the charity football game between the Warriors and the Guardians. She hadn't stayed long because her heart just couldn't handle it. She had abruptly left, crying all the way to her Uber, then in the Uber until she was falling face first on the couch until her tears dried up.

Deep inside she wanted so badly to talk to her mother about what was going on with her and Adam, but she remained silent. Her mom had enough on her plate and Angelina didn't need to pile more on with her own mess of a life. It made her sad wishing she and her mother had that kind of relationship, but they didn't. They never had, really. The only person in this world that knew Angelina the best wasn't her mother, it was Adam.

Angelina held back tears as she listened to her mother talk about her new job and how Dan, the bastard, approved. Suddenly something flickered through her mind as her mom talked about Dan and it scared her initially. Was she more like her mother than she thought? Maggie Adam's always had a man in her life but could never make one relationship work. Dan had been the longest to stick around. Was she going to go through relationship after relationship hoping to find one that would last? As soon as that thought flickered, it was gone because she knew she wasn't anything like her mother. If it wasn't Adam Pride in her life, she was destined to be alone. Her love for that man went that deep.

"Angelina?" Her mother calling her name had her eyes snapping back into focus. "What's wrong?"

"Nothing." Angelina replied but knew her mother wasn't buying it.

"You look so sad." She frowned, then reached out and touched her hand. "I know I haven't been a good mother to you, but know I am here for you if you ever need me."

Once again, she was having something thrown in her face that she wished she could have had all along. First Adam with a text every single night asking about her welfare and now her mother being a real mother, or at least trying. Was the universe so cruel?

"I'm just tired." Angelina replied giving her mom's hand a squeeze. Still not comfortable talking about her and Adam she changed the subject. "I do have some news to share. I've decided instead of nursing I want to be a paramedic. I've been studying nonstop. I took my certification test yesterday and now just waiting for the results. It's been pretty stressful, but I did it."

"Angelina, that's wonderful." Her mother smiled a real smile that Angelina remembered from her childhood when things were…somewhat better between them. "I know whatever you decide to do you will be the best. I've never had to worry about you because you've always been so strong and dedicated to whatever you put your mind to. No mother could ask for a better daughter."

"Thanks mom." Angelina replied feeling tears burn the back of her eyes. Now she felt like a total ass for being a bitch to her mom. "That means a lot to me."

She just nodded as a sad smile formed on her lips. Her mom looked away to stare out the window before saying anything more. "Did Adam ever tell you what he did for me?"

Okay that was out of the blue and confused Angelina. "No, I don't think so."

"He asked me not to tell you because it was a surprise." Her mother said, then turned her head toward her. "He showed up one day, after you left him. He gave me a key."

"A key?" Angelina frowned with a shake of her head. "To what?"

Her mother didn't answer right away, just sat there staring at her from behind those damn sunglasses. "A house." She finally said. "He told me that anytime I needed a place to stay that I could go there to feel safe when Dan was drinking heavy. I was to let him know so he didn't show up to work on it. I only went once."

"What house?" Angelina swallowed the knot that formed in her throat.

"The house he was fixing up for you?" She replied then tilted her head. "I would have thought you'd know by now."

Angelina was speechless. A house...for her...for them? She had no idea.

Slowly her mother removed the sunglasses. "Adam showed up a week ago, Angelina. He told me that he needed the key back, that he was staying at the house to work on it. He then gave me the key to the apartment saying that I could go there if I needed somewhere to go."

Angelina stared at her mother's black and greenish swollen eyes as they stared into hers.

"He had the same sad look on his face as you do right now. I didn't ask what was going on and he didn't say." Her mother said, her voice low for her ears only. "But I know that look, Angelina. Heartbreak is hard to hide, I see it every single time I look into the mirror, and I don't want to see it in yours. That man loves you and I know you love him, have loved him for a very long time."

Angelina was shocked. She had never told her mother her earlier feelings for Adam before they actually got together.

"Honey, I'm your mother. No matter what has happened in our lives I have always been your mother and mothers know things." She answered to Angelina's shocked expression. "I love you. Don't make the mistakes I've made in my life by letting the good one go. You have to fight for what you want as long as it makes you happy. I know that sounds funny coming from me with my situation, but it's my life. Right now we are talking about you."

There was so much her mother didn't know; but one of the most important things at the moment Angelina was going to take away from this conversation was that for the first time in such a long time her mother was being the mother Angelina always wanted. Standing she moved and slid in next to her mom and took her into her arms.

"I love you, mom." Angelina whispered as tears slipped down her cheek. "I'm so sorry for being such a bitch to you."

"Never be sorry for speaking your truth." She whispered, then pulled away with a frown. "Just don't be such a bitch when you're doing it, especially to your mother."

Angelina smiled a genuine smile for the first time in what seemed like forever. "Yes, ma'am."

Her mother laughed giving her another hug. "Come on, let's go get our nails done or something girly. I got some extra cash and I'm treating."

Nodding Angelina stood grabbing her bag then followed her mom out of the coffee shop. Her excitement dimmed somewhat realizing she couldn't recall the last time she and her mother had done anything together other than getting a fast cup of coffee since she had moved out. That had been maybe four times. Yeah, the universe had been a cruel bitch lately and it was making her very nervous.

CHAPTER 2

*a*dam sat at the table focused on his food. His shift had just ended, and he was in a foul mood. Conversation went on around him, but he paid no attention to what was being said. Taking a drink of coffee his eyes met Jill's who was staring at him.

Steve was still talking about the football game between the Warriors and Guardians that happened weeks ago. Adam ignored him, but Jill's constant glaring was harder for him to ignore because she irritated the shit out of him.

"What?" He said in a nasty tone hoping to scare her away, then regretted saying anything at all immediately. Most would back off by his tone, but this was Jill. She didn't back off of anything. Fuck, he really didn't need any shit today.

"You look like shit." Jill said proving his thoughts right.

He just raised his eyebrows then continued to eat ignoring her. That was another thing he should have known wouldn't stop

Jill. He could get up and walk out, but she would follow his ass off a fucking cliff to have her say.

"And your attitude sucks." Jill continued and Adam realized the room became silent.

"Is there a point to your observation, Jill?" Adam dropped his fork to glare at her. "Because if there isn't I really want to eat in peace without your annoying ass commentary about my looks and attitude." Adam growled then cursed when Steve walked over and sat down.

"Jill, give him a break, man." Steve sighed shaking his head at her. "He's going through some shit right now."

"Thanks." Adam mumbled to Steve but should have known Steve had more to add.

"Though she is right, dude." Steve wrinkled his nose. "You are looking like shit, and your attitude..." Steve paused as if looking for the right word.

"Sucks." Jill repeated her earlier observation helping Steve out.

"You did hang up on me...twice." Steve frowned looking hurt by the fact. "Then sent me directly to voicemail after that."

"You're kidding me, right?" Adam sighed running his hand through his hair. "You called me five fucking times in an hour asking me if I was okay."

"Well excuse the fuck out of me for being a good friend and worrying about you." Steve huffed throwing his arms out. "We care about your dumbass."

"Yeah, well don't" Adam pushed his plate away, his appetite gone. "You want to help me?"

"Yeah!" Steve said with a nod.

"Then leave me the fuck alone." Adam growled noticing the kitchen had emptied except for them three. "I'm fine, man."

Steve snorted shaking his head. "You are far from fine friend."

Adam started to stand to get the hell out of there, but Jill shoved the table pinning him between the table and the wall. "You are going to listen to me." Jill leaned over the table glaring at Adam. "I have to work with you. What happened last night cannot happen again, Adam."

"What happened?" Steve asked his eyes widening as he looked from Jill to Adam, then back to Jill again. "What the fuck happened?"

"You want to tell him, or shall I?" Jill tilted her head staring at Adam.

"The asshole deserved every hit I dealt." Adam snarled his eyes narrowing.

"Dammit, why do I always miss the good stuff?" Steve grumbled looking between Jill and Adam.

"You lost control, Adam." Jill ignored Steve. "I had to use my powers to pull you off him."

"Damn, what did the dude do?" Steve frowned when neither of them spoke. "I mean he deserved it…right?"

"He shoulder checked Adam as we were walking through the bar." Jill finally said.

"He…shoulder checked you? That's it?" Steve's eyes widened. "You beat the fuck out of some dude who shoulder checked you in a crowded bar? It was crowded, wasn't it?"

"No, it wasn't." Jill answered still staring at Adam.

"Well, fuck. Okay then please tell me he was vampire and not human." Steve crossed his fingers waiting for the answer to that question.

"Of course he was vampire. I'm not stupid." Adam growled then glared at Jill when she snorted. Adam admitted to himself that he had absolutely lost control and if Jill hadn't been there, he probably would have killed the son of a bitch for a damn shoulder check. "It won't happen again."

"I hope not." Jill frowned then sighed. "I don't want to have to go to Sloan so don't make me, Adam."

"Cross my heart." He made an X over his heart with a smirk then stood. "You've gotten bossy. A little big for your britches."

Jill rolled her eyes then smirked back. "Just watching out for my friend, Adam. That's it."

"I know and I appreciate it." Adam said, then headed for the door. "I'm fine, guys. I'll see you at training later."

Adam walked out of the kitchen his fake smile fading from his face as the lie he just sprouted fell flat. He had heard it and he knew his friends had heard it. He wasn't fine. He was fucked up and if it wouldn't have been for Jill, he would have killed that man last night. Glancing at his phone he walked out of the compound then forced himself to put his phone in his pocket as he climbed onto his bike. It was too early to text Angelina and yet that's all he wanted to do just to make sure she was okay. Every single night he sent a text, and she texted back with a short two-word text of 'I'm fine.' Never anything more, but what did he expect. Hell, he was lucky she even responded. He didn't deserve the response, nor did he deserve her.

As he sat there on his bike just staring at nothing, he felt numb. Something within him had changed and he didn't know what or why. Or maybe he did know why and didn't want to face it. Fuck, he was messed up in the head. Pulling his phone out again he sighed. He had promised Tessa he would stop by before training. It was the last thing he wanted to do, but he knew if he didn't, she would give him hell and he just wasn't up for that. The only thing he felt like doing was finding bad guys and beating their asses. Took his mind off things. In all honesty what he really wanted to do was find Angelina and beg for her forgiveness but knew he wouldn't do that. Not yet anyway. He needed to make sure he was worthy enough to earn that forgiveness and right now he wasn't sure he was. With a curse he took off knowing the only thing that could calm him was a quick fast ride.

The ride wasn't long enough to take the edge off. He was already pulling up to Jared and Tessa's, his mood darker than before. Parking behind Tessa's car he got off and started toward the old porch. He slowed letting the memories of sitting with Gramps run through his mind. They would sit on that old porch for hours while Gramps talked about the good old days. Damn Adam missed him, missed the stories.

Giving a knock he opened the door and walked inside. "Tess." Adam called out just as the smell of apple pie hit his senses.

"Kitchen." Tessa yelled out just as Adam entered.

"I sure hope you made that for me." Adam went to pinch a piece of crust, but Tessa stopped him with a smack of a potholder.

"It's not." Jared said coming inside. "It's for me, but I'll share."

Adam had heard Jared ride up. He had a feeling this was an intervention of sorts and Tessa had called in her Mate for backup.

Frowning Adam shook his head. "I take it you didn't invite me over for apple pie."

Jared held his hands up. "Not part of this. Your sister wants to talk to you and I'm getting my pie and leaving. This is between the two of you." Jared kissed Tessa on the cheek and took his plate of pie before turning back to Adam. "Though I do suggest you listen Adam."

"Yeah." Adam sighed still taking the pie. If he was going to have to sit through listening to his sister bitch at him, he might as well eat.

"Upset her and I'll kick your ass." Jared warned before walking out leaving them alone.

Adam smirked than sat at the table and started in on the huge piece of pie. He knew Tessa sat across from him, but he didn't look up from his plate. "I've got things under control sis."

"Do you?" Tessa responded not sounding so sure.

"Tessa, I love you, but this is none of your business." Adam sighed pushing the empty plate away after inhaling his piece.

"You broke her heart, Adam." Tessa continued as if she didn't hear him though he knew she did hear him but didn't give a damn.

"Don't you think I know that." Adam tried to keep his voice calm, but the anger coming out of his mouth proved that he failed to do that.

"I honestly don't know what to think, Adam." Tessa remained calm as she stared at him and what killed him most was there was no judgement in her eyes, only confusion. Well hell, she might as well join the club because he had never been more confused in his life than he was right now. "We used to be close. You don't talk to me anymore."

Adam rubbed his eyes in frustration. "A lot has happened in our lives, sis. We both know things change."

"Only if you let them change." Tessa cocked her eyebrow at him. "And you are right about one thing."

"Excuse me?" Adam removed his hands from his eyes. "Did you just say I'm right?"

"Don't get used to it and only on one thing." Tessa rolled her eyes. "Your relationship with Angelina is none of my business, but I wouldn't be a good sister not to realize that your heart is also broken. And I'm worried about you."

Adam swallowed hard and didn't respond right away. He didn't deserve her worry. Not at all. "Don't be." He finally said. "Angelina is mine. I just have things to work through." He added more than he intended to. Tessa had a way of reading between the lines.

"Angelina is a beautiful, bright woman. If you're not careful Adam, she may not be yours for long." Tessa didn't pull any punches.

Deep rage boiled inside him at that thought, but he remained silent.

"Now that was me being the nice sister." Tessa grabbed his plate and stood. "Now the bitch sister is coming out. You need to grow up and get your shit together. Marriage between two people should be cherished and not thrown away just because you have things to work through. It's selfish and a bunch of bullshit. Nothing about this is fair to Angelina. Man up, Adam because you are very close to losing the best thing that has ever happened to you. You treated her like shit once when you were both very young and she forgave you. Once again you are doing the same thing and she isn't that young naïve girl anymore. Your Angel may just use her wings brother."

"Are you finished?" Adam heard every single word like it was a knife to his heart, but she didn't understand. No one understood. He was protecting her, dammit.

Turning toward the sink she slammed the plate into the sink. Adam was surprised it didn't break. She turned back around, her face stern and sad at the same time. "Actually, no I'm not finished." She faced him. "You are nothing like our father so stop acting like him, Adam."

Even though those words were like a slap to the face Adam realized he was wrong. One person did understand, and it was Tessa. And she was right, he was acting like their father and that, from a very young age, had been a true fear of his. When he didn't respond to that Tessa frowned.

"That's it isn't it?" Tessa stepped toward him in concern, but Adam scooted the chair back and stood up. "Adam you are nothing like Frank. I shouldn't have said that."

"But you did and yes, there are times I see him in me. You can call him Frank from here on out, but that doesn't take away the fact we both have his fucking blood running through us." Adam spat out more harshly than he wanted.

"As does our mothers' who was a sweet soul." Tessa responded without hesitation. "And that is the only blood I will claim."

Tessa was more like their mother than he could ever be. Things she did, said and her reactions reminded him so much of their mom it hurt sometimes and had him missing her. But on the flip side he did and said things that reminded him of his old man which meant that the hate he felt for his bastard of a father turned into self-hatred. His moods could turn dark quickly, his thoughts at times were selfish and sometimes he felt himself falling deeper into those moods and thoughts, accepting them because it was easier than fighting.

His eyes rose to meet Tessa who remained silent as she stared at him. "I should have never killed him, Tess." Adam finally admitted to someone rather than keeping those thoughts shoved into the dark recesses of his own mind. "Even though he deserved having his fucking throat ripped out, it shouldn't have been me."

CHAPTER 3

*J*ake sat on his motorcycle; light snow had begun to fall but he paid little attention to the white flakes landing on his leather jacket. His fingers absently went up to the chain around his neck as he touched the wedding ring that had once belonged to Tracy. The vision of her shimmered in his mind but faded quickly. Lately her image was more shadows than details and he didn't understand why. His time at the cemetery had also dwindled from every single day, sometimes more than once to once or twice a week. The guilt he felt at times almost brought him to his knees.

With a curse he let go of the ring as he climbed off his bike. He climbed the steps to the VC compound knowing what he had to do but felt like a fucking traitor for doing it. "Damn." He cursed as he heard the door buzz before he could use the code. All Guardians had the code for the compound now. Glancing up at the camera he gave a nod to whoever let him in.

As soon as he stepped through the door, he heard Sloan and Charger talking in Sloan's office. Heading that way, he walked in shutting the door behind him.

"This must be important." Charger frowned at Jake.

Glancing around he wanted to make sure they were alone. He saw Sloan's Mate Becky in the back at her desk, but she was busy on the computer.

"If you are here to quit you can walk your ass right back out that door you just closed." Charger shook his head as if emphasizing what he just said.

Jake looked at Charger and once again felt like a traitor but knew this was exactly what needed to be done or he would be doing exactly what Charger just insinuated. Jake then looked to Sloan. "I want a full transfer to the Warriors."

The room became deathly silent. He even heard the tapping of the keyboard from Becky's computer stop. Jake's gaze went back to Charger who showed no expression on his face.

"Jake I'd be more than happy to have you as part of the VC, but only if Charger is in full agreement to releasing you from the Guardians." Sloan answered while Charger said nothing. "Can I ask why the transfer. We are working together now as one team."

He knew that Sloan probably thought there was an issue with Charger, but that wasn't it. He glanced over his shoulder his eyes meeting Becky's who quickly took the hint and stood up. As she passed him, she touched Jake's arm lightly as if she knew the answer to Sloan's question. He watched as she opened the door and walked out shutting it softly behind her.

"It's just something I have to do. If I want to keep doing this, I have to…" Jake started to explain and yet the words just stuck in his throat.

"He has my full support." Charger said as Jake's words trailed off. "I'll sign the transfer papers now."

Jake didn't know exactly how to feel about Charger's full agreement to his transfer. Relief or like he got kicked in the balls. "Thanks." Was all Jake could manage to say at the moment.

"You don't have to explain anything to us, Jake." Charger gave him a nod. "Even though I hate to lose you as a Guardian, I support you. I'd rather have you on a team than not. And I know if I don't approve this transfer you'll walk."

"I will still have loyalty to the Guardians." Jake finally managed to say as Sloan got up to head toward Becky's area to grab the transfer papers. "Thank you, Charger. This isn't personal."

"I know it's not." Charger assured him, then took the papers from Sloan and signed them. "Plus, with Daniel it will be good to have you here. He still has a lot of questions, and you can still feed us the information he gives you."

"That will be good for Daniel." Sloan agreed with a nod.

Jake nodded just glad he hadn't really had to go into an explanation on why this transfer had to happen. Sometimes he didn't understand it himself. He just knew since Tracy's death things were different for him and the memories being around the Guardians were too painful for him to deal with. It was either transfer or like Charger said, walk. If he walked away from the only thing he was good at Jake knew he wouldn't last long. Charger handed Jake the paper and pen after he signed it.

Putting it on Sloan's desk he glanced at Charger's signature, then quickly signed his own pushing it to Sloan. "I appreciate it." Jake said looking at Sloan. "You will have the same loyalty I give the Guardians."

"Never thought to question it." Sloan signed his own name before looking at Jake. "Welcome to the shitshow."

That statement managed to put a half grin on Jake's face. "Guess I'll feel right at home since that's exactly what I'm leaving."

"That is the fucking truth." Charger snorted with a chuckle. "You tell Kane yet?"

"No." Jake replied with a frown not looking forward to that confrontation.

"Good luck with that." Charger cocked his eyebrow as he slapped Jake on the back before leaving Sloan's office. "You need anything Jake, you know where I am and know you will always be welcomed back if Sloan's too much of a dick to deal with."

"Fuck you, Charger." Sloan said just as the door closed.

A grin slipped across Jake's lips as Charger left the room, but then faded quickly. He was a little surprised Charger took him asking for a transfer so well, then again, he really shouldn't be. They were probably tired of babysitting him just in case he decided to off himself. In truth those thoughts were still with him but had faded over time.

"Did you just get off shift?" Sloan asked after a long moment of silence.

"No." Jake responded ready to get to work. He didn't like to be still long, when he was off shift with the Guardians, he usually teamed up with someone to help out. "I'm ready to work."

Sloan gave him an approving nod as he texted something on his phone. "I'd like to team you up with Daniel, but he's not free today. Adam is getting ready to go out on shift with Jill and Steve. I'll send you with them."

"Sounds good." Jake answered not caring who he went with as long as he kept busy.

"Raven just came off shift or I'd team you with her." Sloan said absently as he continued to stare at his phone.

"I'd rather you not." Jake's voice was even, unemotional.

Sloan glanced up from his phone at that response. "You got problems with Raven?"

"No." Jake answered honestly. He didn't have a problem with Raven, but he knew her well and until things settled with him transferring, he just wasn't up to answering the million questions she would have.

Sloan stared at him a little longer before looking away as Adam walked in the door. Jake was relieved because he honestly was done talking and ready to work.

"What's up?" Adam asked Sloan before looking at Jake with a nod.

"I'm sending Jake out with you, Jill, and Steve tonight. During slow times show Jake the areas we patrol even when off duty, so he knows. If you have any informants introduce them to Jake." Sloan ordered with authority.

"Sure." Adam said, then frowned glancing back at Jake. "You transferred?"

Jake nodded but remained silent.

"Cool." Adam said then stuck out his hand giving Jake a quick shake of welcome. "Glad to have you. Okay, let's get going before Jill sends Steve in here to see what's going on."

"Yes, please do." Sloan sighed with narrowed eyes. "I haven't wanted to kill anyone yet today and sure as shit that will change if that fucker walks through the door."

"What fucker we talking about?" Steve popped in at that moment. Talk about timing. When no one said anything, Steve shrugged then looked at Adam. "Come on dude, Jill's talking about hot wiring your car again. She's ready to go."

"Dammit." Adam cursed then looked at Sloan. "Can we do an even trade? Him for Jill?"

"Him who?" Steve frowned looking confused as he glanced at Jake. "You?"

"He's transferring." Adam informed Steve as he made a phone call. "Hot wire my car and die. Give us two minutes dammit." He hung up the phone.

Jake grinned at Adam's short call to Jill. This definitely wasn't going to be a boring night. Steve walked up and was staring at him with a huge smirk on his face. "What?"

"It was the football game, wasn't it?" Steve said nodding his head as if agreeing with himself. "I knew it. Sloan, get the transfer papers ready because after that ass kicking we gave them they are going to be coming in droves."

"We were actually tied." Jake reminded him with a cocked eyebrow.

"That's right we were." Steve said still nodding like an idiot. "Then I made that amazing touchdown."

Steve started to do the Ickey shuffle, but Sloan's loud growl stopped him in mid-step. "I swear if you fucking do that shit one more time in my sight, I will first tear your legs off and then beat the fuck out of you with them."

Adam grabbed Steve by the back of the shirt and hauled him out of the office. "Head out to the parking lot when you're done, Jake."

Jake laughed shaking his head then looked toward Sloan. "Thanks for giving me a shot, Sloan."

"Yeah, save the thanks for later after you spend hours with those three. They're good Warriors, but a pain in my fucking ass." Sloan snorted, then gave Jake a nod of dismissal.

Jake walked out only to see Charger leaning against the wall across from Sloan's office. With a frown he stopped. "You waiting for me?"

"Just wanted you to know I understand what you have to do. Letting you transfer isn't easy, but to keep you in this line of business I knew it's what needed to happen." Charger pushed off the wall, then gave Jake a brotherly hug. "Just watch your ass out there."

"Thanks Charger." Jake pulled away. "You're a good man."

"Yeah, don't know about all that." Charger chuckled with a cocked eyebrow. "Record your conversation with Kane if I'm not there. I really want to see him lose his shit."

Jake frowned when Charger laughed slapping him on the back as he headed deeper into the compound. Turning to look at Charger over his shoulder Jake called out, "I take that back." Jake said, then snarled. "You're a dick."

"I knew you would." Charger continued to chuckle. "And yes, I am."

"Fucker." Jake mumbled as he headed out of the compound into the parking lot where Jill, Adam and Steve waited. Jill and Adam were arguing on who was going to drive while Steve was staring at him with a knowing grin as he did that stupid ass shuffle across the parking lot. Instantly he had second thoughts on what he had just done. What in the fuck had he walked into willingly?

CHAPTER 4

*A*ngelina hadn't slept but maybe an hour. After getting her nails done with her mom, which had been surprisingly pleasant, she received a text saying to be at the firehouse by eight to do her first ride along. Nerves had plagued her all night as did the excitement of something new, something she was hopefully good at.

After she was ready, three hours early, she paced around the apartment. She had texted her mom telling her that she had her first ride along, but no text was returned. She checked her phone once again to see, but still nothing. Feeling a little disappointed she had no one to share her nerves or excitement with. Grabbing a bowl, she forced down some cereal as she watched the news which was as depressing as usual. Nothing good happened in the world anymore.

Glancing at the time she hurried and washed her bowl, grabbed her bag, and headed out the door. The firehouse was close, so she decided to walk. No reason to waste money on an

Uber. Her money was running low, and she still had to pay half her rent in a few days. Where she could save, she saved.

Locking the door behind her she headed down the steps zipping her coat. Her gaze scanned the area but didn't see Adam anywhere. She never knew when he would show up just to sit up the road. Today she pushed the disappointment of not seeing him deep inside where she kept her hurt and continued on her way.

The air was brisk nipping at her bare neck and ears. She had braided her long blonde hair to keep it out of her way while she worked. There were times she thought of cutting it off, but always chickened out. She liked her long hair, just not when she was working. A man was coming her way causing her body to stiffen as she continued. She glanced at the other side of the street thinking maybe she should cross but decided against it. Ever since the day two men attacked her on the way to meet Jill, Katrina, and Mira she had been much more cautious on where and when she walked anywhere.

Thankfully the man passed without even looking her way. Breathing a sigh of relief, she continued. Everyone was putting up their Christmas decorations making the street look festive. She had spent Thanksgiving alone and it looked as if she would be spending Christmas alone also. Bev, her roommate, had left the day before Thanksgiving to visit her family in Texas. She had been invited to go but declined because of her new job. Her mom never invited her for Thanksgiving, and she knew that her asshole of a stepfather had been home. Angelina didn't blame her mom and honestly, she probably would have declined anyway. Who was she kidding, she would have flat out refused.

So she had spent Thanksgiving in the small apartment with a pizza with pineapple, beer and old movies. She hated it. Spilled a few tears and then went to bed. Christmas would be worse which is why if she is able to, she will work around the clock Christmas Eve and Christmas Day. Adam still texted her every night, but she hadn't really seen him since the football game. She'd hear a motorcycle pass the apartment, but never saw if it was Adam or not. Her stomach rolled thinking about him and their situation.

Spotting the firehouse up ahead she shook those feelings aside and picked up her pace. She was only a half an hour early, which was fine. Better early than late. Finding the door, she walked inside.

"Can I help you?" A man asked as soon as she walked inside.

"I'm Angelina...Pride." Angelina replied since she still legally had Adam's last name. "I'm here to see Lonnie Jones."

"Sure thing." He smiled then picked up the phone on the wall. "Lonnie, you have a young lady here to see you. Angelina Pride."

Angelina looked around what seemed to be a small lobby area. It definitely wasn't welcoming, and she wondered if any women worked here. It sure could use a woman's touch.

"I'll do it." The man said then hung up the phone. He turned toward Angelina. "Lonnie wants me to bring you back. I'm Ben. It's nice to meet you Angelina and welcome aboard."

"Thanks, Ben." Angelina gave him a smile as she followed him through the door and down a hallway. "I'm still waiting for my test scores, but they asked me to do a ride along today."

"That's protocol." Ben replied holding another door open for her. "I will tell you we are in desperate need for more paramedics and EMT's. Lonnie is a good man. He will make sure you're taken care of."

"Are you a firefighter?" Angelina asked the older man. He was at least in his fifties, but in amazing shape.

"Yes, ma'am." Ben beamed proudly then glanced at his watch. "Retiring in one week, three days, four hours and fifty….six minutes."

"Down to the minutes." Angelina chuckled when he nodded. "Do you have big plans for retirement? Florida maybe? Disney Land?"

"Grandkids." He said with a sparkle in his eyes. "Spend every minute I can with my grandkids."

Angelina never knew her grandparents and felt a ping of jealousy, but realized how silly that was as well as how sick and tired she was of having damn pity parties for herself. She needed to buck up and get over things instead of dwelling on them. "Then Disney Land may be in your future."

This time he knocked on a door, then opened it. "That is very true. Here you go, Angelina." She stepped back so she could enter. "Let me know if you need anything."

Thanking him she turned to see Lonnie, who interviewed her, sitting behind his desk. He was middle aged, with dark graying hair and ruddy cheeks. His smile was friendly and comforting making her feel at ease instantly. A very good trait to have when dealing with ill or hurt people. She on the other hand was just nervous and yet, she felt instantly at ease.

"Hello, Angelina." Lonnie said pointing toward a chair in front of his desk. "Have a seat."

Angelina did, setting her bag on the floor. "How was your Thanksgiving?" She felt she needed to start with the pleasantry before asking for him to let her work all the time.

"It was good until it wasn't." Lonnie answered honestly, then laughed at the confused look on her face. "I was scheduled off, my first scheduled day off in months and well, right in the middle of dinner I was called in. Car accident with multiple injuries."

"Oh, I'm sorry." Angelina felt like kicking herself now for even asking.

"Don't be. It's my life, the life I chose." Lonnie chuckled. "How about you? Did you have a good Thanksgiving?"

"It was...good." She lied. It sucked but felt his sucked more since he had to deal with hurt and maybe even dead accident victims. Hers was just feeling sorry for herself bull crap she had to deal with.

"Good, huh?" Lonnie chuckled obviously knowing a lie when he heard one.

"Could have been better." Angelina grinned liking Lonnie's infectious good-natured chuckle. "Christmas looks to be just as jolly, so I'll go ahead and let you know I am free to work around the clock if needed."

Lonnie's smile faded slightly as he stared at her. "I'll keep that in mind. Hopefully your test scores will come in soon, but until then I will have you ride along. Learn as much as you can during that time. You can help, but no administering medical care unless it is a life and death situation. In that case we will figure it out afterwards."

Angelina nodded even though she knew that rule already.

"Things have changed in our field. Things you've seen on television, movies or in real life are obsolete. Soon even the tests will be scrapped. As long as someone knows medical care they will be accepted. We are overwhelmed with calls from car accidents and sickness to vampire attacks to possession."

Listening closely Angelina remained silent. None of this surprised her in the least.

Cocking his head Lonnie tapped his pen on the desk. "Most new employees have some emotion to what I just told you. What don't I know about you, Angelina Pride."

Angelina's eyes shifted away for a second as she straightened her sleeves, she then looked back up at him. She really hadn't wanted to expose her personal life at all, but she knew she needed to be honest. No doubt she was going to run into the Warriors while doing her job, it was a given. Lonnie was going to find out sooner rather than later. "Adam Pride is my husband." Angelina began and decided not to mention their separation for now. Her employer didn't need to know that much of her business outside of work. "

"Adam Pride." Lonnie's frown deepened as his pen tapped faster before his eyes widened slightly. "Wasn't he the quarterback for the VC Warriors during the charity football game?"

"Yes." Angelina nodded wanting to change the subject, but by the look on Lonnie's face that wasn't going to happen.

"Hell of a football game. Watching them throwing each other around on that field." Lonnie chuckled shaking his head. "It was a sight to see. And that Warrior who did the Ickey shuffle on the winning touchdown was classic."

Angelina actually did smile at that. She had seen clips on television of Steve making the touchdown and delighting the Cincinnati crowd with the famous Ickey shuffle. "So do you work closely with the Warriors?"

"We do if we are going into a highly volatile vampire situation." Lonnie replied becoming a little more serious as he changed gears from the football game to work. "We have a few vampires on payroll, but not enough to ride with all the units so some are without protection, that's when we call in the Warriors."

Angelina nodded knowing that this could be a possibility, but there were a lot of Warriors. What was the chance of Adam being called in with her unit. Knowing her luck she snorted, high. Very high chance that it will be Adam. Her heart fluttered at the thought, and she cursed to herself. This was going to be her career and if she had to face Adam every once in a while, so be it, she was a professional and could handle it. That's what her brain was telling her, but her heart was saying something entirely different.

CHAPTER 5

⌒∾

*A*dam walked around the building alert to his surroundings. Jill said she saw movement as they passed, but so far, he had found nothing. This was one of the well-known areas for rogues to squat while waiting for unsuspecting victims. This part of town had so many empty rundown buildings that Sloan had petitioned the city to tear them down, but the refusals to do so kept coming in claiming the money just wasn't there. Crimson Rush operations also seemed to pop up even after the Warriors had cleaned them out. It was an endless cycle to an endless crisis overwhelming not only them but every city in the world.

"Anything?" Adam asked as Jake walked toward him from the other direction. Jake was a pretty cool dude. He didn't say much but knew exactly what the hell he was doing. Adam hadn't had much interaction with him before today, but yeah, he liked the guy. He would definitely be a valuable asset to the team. He did however wonder why he would transfer but figured one day the truth would come out. Right now, he felt like it wasn't any of his business and just like he didn't enjoy people prying in his personal shit he himself wouldn't pry in others.

"No." Jake said glancing at the building. "Jill and Steve still in there?"

Before Adam could respond a loud crash came from inside the building. Neither Jake nor Adam hesitated as they took off at full speed. Adam followed Jake who was in front of him jumping down a flight of steps where the sounds of struggle and cursing were coming from.

Adam slid to a stop as he watched a vampire leap toward Jill who was already fighting off another one. Steve had his hands full with three of his own and was no help to Jill. Jake leaped into action heading to help Jill as Adam ran and slid taking out one of the three attacking Steve.

"They're not rogue." Steve yelled telling them something they already knew.

Adam slammed the vampire who he had taken down, then grabbed the knife out of his pocket and sliced the fucker's throat. He glanced quickly to see how Jill and Jake were fairing just in time to see Jake break one of the bastards neck. Jill was throwing her guy around using her power and seemed to be enjoying it immensely as she cursed at him. A sudden feeling of fear overcame him as many mixed emotions took control over his senses. Adam slowly turned, his eyes searching. They weren't alone.

Seeing a darkened hallway, he moved quickly that way, but remained aware of his surroundings. The closer he got the emotions were hitting him like rocks in the chest. At the end of the short hallway was ten small children huddled up together staring at him with so much fear it had him cursing.

"Keep one alive!" He ordered loudly over his shoulder then turned back to the children and knelt. "You're safe now. Just stay right here and I'll be right back."

"How do we know you're not one of them?" One boy who looked a little older than the rest tried to sound brave and unafraid, which gained respect from Adam.

"All I can do is give you my word that you are safe." Adam responded looking at each of them. "Now stay here and don't move. I'll be back."

Adam stood as they all nodded except for the older boy who still looked unsure. Good. It was an evil world; the kid should be weary especially after what they had just gone through. Turning he walked back down the hallway. His gaze scanned the area to see Steve leaning against the wall holding his bleeding arm, then to Jill who had blood pouring from a gaping wound in her neck and then to Jake who held the remaining bastard by the throat against the wall.

"He still breathing?" Adam asked as he walked closer.

"For now." Jake growled not taking his eyes off their prisoner. "Fucker ripped her throat before I could stop him. You need to call Slade. She's losing a lot of blood and the wound isn't closing as quick as it should."

"Fuck!" Adam pulled out his phone, sent an urgent text to the one number none of them ever wanted to use. It was an alert to all Warriors that a Warrior was down.

"I'm fine." Jill's voice sounded weak as she slid down a wall. "Just resting my legs for a minute."

37

Adam took off his shirt, which wasn't the most sanitary, but it was all he had. Kneeling he pressed it against the wound applying pressure. She hissed but allowed him to do it. He then looked toward Steve. "You good?"

"I'll live." Steve said sounding pissed.

"Good." Adam gave a nod toward the hallway. "There's a bunch of scared kids down that hallway."

"On it." Steve pushed himself off the wall hurrying in the direction Adam motioned.

Turning his attention back to Jill who had her eyes closed he frowned. "Jill?"

"Yeah?" Jill answered immediately, but kept her eyes closed.

"Stay awake." Adam ordered not liking the coloring of her skin. "Slade is on his way."

"I'm good. Just hurts like a bitch and I hate pain. Pisses me off." Jill replied, her voice sounding weak. "Jake after their done questioning that bastard kill him for me."

"I have a feeling Slade will beat me to that." Jake replied still holding the vampire by the throat.

Adam watched as his shirt became quickly soaked with her blood. This wasn't good. Not good at all. Wanting to look to see if the wound was healing more, he was afraid to remove the pressure. "You were always a pussy when it came to pain." Adam decided to try to get Jill to snap out of it a little. He didn't like this Jill. Quiet didn't suit her and it was scaring the shit out of him.

"For once I will agree with you." Jill answered making him grin. "I am definitely a pussy when it comes to pain."

"What the fuck happened?" Adam wanted to keep her talking until Slade got there. If something happened to Jill, he would never forgive himself.

"They must have heard us." Jill started then licked her lips. "Ambushed us. Rushed in before we knew what was happening."

Adam looked down at Jill's shirt covered in blood. This much blood loss even for a vampire was dangerous. Glancing at his phone he sent another text indicating this time the Warrior down was Jill. That should get Slade's ass here. He should have done that in the first fucking place.

"What was Steve doing? Running his mouth too loud again? I've told him when we are scoping out a building to shut the fuck up." Adam said then grinned when a small smile curved her lips. "Tell me he wasn't doing that fucking shuffle right before you guys got attacked."

This time Jill laughed, then coughed as a small spittle of blood spattered her lips. His eyes went directly to Jake who's concerned gaze went from Jill to Adam. They were vampires yes, but Jill was a half-breed before turning full blood. They didn't heal like normal pure blood vampires.

"You got this?" Adam asked Jake feeling an urgency to get Jill out of there.

"Go." Jake ordered his eyes still on Jill. "We got this."

"Jill, I'm going to pick you up. Can you keep pressure on your neck?" Adam asked nervous as fuck. If she wasn't able to do that there was no way he could get her out of there.

"I don't know." Jill's answer didn't come as quick this time. "I think I'm fine. Just let me rest for a minute. I think it's healing."

Adam's eyes went to his shirt which was now completely soaked in Jill's blood. That wound was not healing. Or at least wasn't healing fast enough. "Did the fucker bite her?"

Jake nodded when Adam looked his way. Fuck! He didn't know what in the hell to do. He couldn't let go of the pressure on her neck and they all had their fucking bikes. "Steve!" Jake yelled as the vampire Jake was holding started to put up a fight.

"Yeah?" Steve yelled back.

"Get out here with the kids." Jake called out his eyes on Jill.

Adam turned to see Steve with the kids slowly following him. "I need to get Jill out of here, but I can't carry her and hold pressure on the wound."

"She said she was okay." Steve hurried over concern showing all over his face.

"She lied." Adam motioned for Steve to get on the other side. "Take off your shirt. She's soaked mine. As soon as I remove this one replace it with yours and hold a lot of pressure on that wound."

"Fuck!" Steve said as he took off his shirt then quickly placed it on the wound when Adam took his away. "She really needs to stop fucking lying."

Adam picked Jill up carefully as Steve kept the pressure. Jake was ordering the kids to sit against the wall where he could see them. He now had the vampire in a secure headlock so he could see the children better.

"Jill, you need to wake up." Adam said as they made their way toward the steps. His stomach was in knots sensing the worse was happening.

"I'm awake." Jill mumbled then frowned without opening her eyes. "And I didn't lie, asshole. I'm fine. Just…hate…pain."

Just as they made it to the top of the steps Slade was blasting through the door looking like a killer ready for battle. His eyes snapped to her as he instantly reached for her.

"Wait!" Adam backed away. "She has a bad wound on her neck and it's not healing fast enough. She's already soaked my shirt with blood and is close to soaking Steve's."

"What happened?" Slade said as he went from killer to doctor in an instant. He lifted one of Jill's eyelids and then the other.

"I didn't see it. I was with the kids I found, but Jake said the bastard ripped her throat with his fangs." Adam informed him. Once again Slade became a killer as his eyes quickly narrowed toward the steps before going back to Jill.

"It hurts…Slade." Jill whispered through dry lips.

"I know, babe. I'm going to make it better." Slade said as his eyes narrowed. "The blood on her lips? Is that splatter?"

When Adam didn't answer right away Slade's eyes snapped to his. "No, she coughed, and the blood came from her mouth." Adam saw something flash in Slade's eyes that he didn't like. He knew he could easily read Slade to find out what it meant but didn't want to. His fear for Jill overwhelmed his wanting to know.

Slade slowly moved the shirt against her neck so he could see the wound. With a low curse he quickly moved it back. "Carefully transfer her to me." He ordered Adam then looked at Steve. "Do not release the pressure on her neck."

"Never." Steve said with a small catch to his throat. There weren't many times you got to see Steve be serious, but this was definitely one of those moments.

As careful as he could Adam transferred Jill into Slade's arms. "Is she going to be okay?" Adam asked, but Slade didn't even acknowledge he heard him. He just turned and rushed out of the building with Steve doing everything he could to stop the bleeding. Adam stood there looking at the empty space where they had been. It wasn't until Sloan appeared did he snap out of it.

"What the hell happened?" Sloan asked, and not in his usual brash tone which was surprising.

"Jake and I were outside doing a perimeter check while Jill and Steve cleared out the building. Nothing suspicious, but this is one of the buildings we check on every two weeks because it's out of the way and we've busted a lot of rogues in this place." Adam stated trying to get his mind off Jill and focused on what he was relaying to Sloan. "From what I understand Jill and Steve were ambushed and were overtaken. We heard a loud crash and took off. It was pretty much three on one. Once things were under control, I heard something down a hallway and went to check it out. That's when I found the kids. When I came back out, I noticed Jill was injured and sent the text."

Warriors had started filing in, every single one of them silent as they passed. Adam knew it was because of their worry for Jill.

"Nicole is on her way." Sloan finally replied as he started down the steps.

Torn with what to do Adam cursed as he stared at the way Slade disappeared with Jill, then down the steps where Sloan disappeared. Knowing there wasn't anything he could do for Jill he turned and followed Sloan. He had a job to do, Slade was doing his. Jill was tough and too much of a mean ass to die. Adam swallowed hard shaking those thoughts away.

"Adam where are they?" Nicole's voice broke him out of his thoughts.

Looking up he saw Nicole coming down behind him with Jessie following her. "Down here." Adam said as he started down the steps again but stopped. "Did you see Jill?"

Nicole's eyes met his as she nodded. "Slade is working on her now."

"An ambulance pulled up just as we were coming in." Jessie informed him with a worried frown. "Slade put her in the ambulance, but they haven't left yet."

"Thanks." Adam nodded, then continued to where the kids were. At least Slade could get her somewhere without having to worry. That made him feel somewhat better. Okay, that was a lie. It didn't make him feel better at all. Jill being so silent and still was not a good sign. He would take full responsibility if...

"I heard he was a good doctor." Jessie said as she passed him. She touched his arm softly. "She's going to be okay."

Adam really didn't know this woman at all, but for some strange reason her words and voice soothed him. It was odd, but honestly where his mind was going anyone giving him reassurance about Jill, he would drink it up. His thoughts went to Angelina, and he knew as soon as he got a free moment he needed to let her know what had happened. She and Jill were close, she deserved to know, and he would be the one to tell her.

CHAPTER 6

*A*ngelina sat in front of the ambulance listening to Rodney talk. A few times she tuned him out because, well, he was boring as hell. He was also a know it all. Yeah, one of those guys. He was nice enough, but definitely not someone she wanted to partner with all the time.

They had been riding for about an hour. So far, the only call that came in was a worried mom with a little boy running a fever. Angelina had stood back and watched Rodney deal with the worried mother did not impress her at all.

"Have you ever done that?" Rodney asked and Angelina had no idea what in the hell he was talking about.

Angelina was looking out the window as she cursed silently. Shit, she had no idea what he had been talking about. Before she could say anything, she spotted VC SUV's and motorcycles outside of a building. Leaning up she stared as the ambulance slowed. News crews were outside the building, and she saw Jax and Blaze keeping them at bay as Duncan talked to the police.

"Looks like the Warriors are busy tonight." Rodney said as they slowly passed.

Her eyes searched for one certain Warrior, her heart pounding as she prayed that he was okay. Suddenly her eyes saw Slade rushing out of the building carrying someone with Steve right beside him holding what looked like a red shirt against the persons neck. She couldn't quite see who it was, but whoever it was they were too small to be Adam. Her heart started beating again until she saw the blue hair.

"Stop!" She ordered Rodney who continued to drive slowly.

"We haven't been called. We don't respond to VC matters unless we are called." Rodney's tone took on that annoying I know what I'm doing and that's that attitude.

"Stop the fucking ambulance." Angelina growled as she opened the door. Thankfully he did stop when she did that and she jumped out. She ran across the sidewalk, just as a cop started to stop her.

"She's fine." Jax called out as Angelina rushed past the officer toward Slade.

"What happened?" Angelina said in rush as she reached them.

"I have to stop the bleeding." Slade said as Angelina looked up at him. The worry and helplessness she saw on his face had her taking over.

"Come on." She led them toward the ambulance where Rodney now stood watching her with an angry expression. She pushed passed him as she opened the back door.

"This is not a good start." Rodney informed her with a frown. "I'm going to have to report this. Lonnie isn't going to be happy."

"Do what you have to do, Rodney." Angelina said as she climbed into the back of the ambulance with Steve and Slade. "But do it out here."

Angelina slid in beside Steve who was holding the cloth against Jill's neck. His hands were shaking as she stared down at Jill. Their eyes met and she saw tears in his. Okay, this was bad. Slade wasn't doing much better as he pulled the cloth away and cursed. Blood was pouring from the nasty wound.

"Oh, God." Steve said, his voice cracking.

Thankfully Rodney had gone over the layout of the ambulance and where everything was. Thankfully she paid attention to his ongoing monotone instruction on where it was and why it was used. He was an EMT, she was a paramedic which meant she was higher in the food chain with her education, but she kept that to herself.

With a calmness she didn't feel she started grabbing things to help stop the bleeding. "How much blood has she lost?"

When neither Slade, who took over applying pressure, or Steve didn't say anything she stopped and looked at them both. Steve finally looked up at her.

"She soaked Adam's shirt." Steve said, then looked down at the cloth. "That's mine."

Angelina glanced at Slade who was checking her pupils. "Thanks Steve. We got it from here."

Steve nodded as he backed out of the ambulance and closed the door. Her gaze went back to Slade. She had seen this before. Slade was one of the best doctors she had ever seen, but this was Jill. His Mate. Once he was over the shock of seeing her like this the doctor in him would kick in, but until then she needed to take control.

"Can I?" She touched his hand, but he refused to move his hand away. "Slade, I know we have to keep pressure on the wound, but we also need to see what is going on. Do you know if there was an artery sliced? I know she's a vampire, but I also know she's said she doesn't heal the same as a pure blood."

"Fuck!" Slade cursed as he removed the shirt and tossed it.

Angelina kept her gasp to herself as she really got a good look at the wound. She watched as he examined it, ready with a thick sterile gauze to replace Steve's blood-soaked shirt. Angelina touched Jill's forehead. It was so cold to the touch. Her stomach rolled in panic but she outwardly remained calm.

"No, it doesn't look like the artery was hit and the bleeding seems to be slowing." Slade continued his examination. "But she's lost so much already and losing anymore could be…"

Even though he let his sentence trail off she knew what he meant. It could be deadly to Jill who was so small anyway.

"But it's not healing fast enough." Slade said absently as he took the gauze from her and placed it on her neck. "I need to get her to take my blood and the hospital is too fucking far."

There was a loud banging on the door before it swung open. "Okay, this is enough, Angelina. Lonnie is on his way. I need you to get out of my ambulance."

The growl that came out of Slade had Angelina scooting back and by the looks of it had Rodney shitting his pants. "Get the fuck away from this ambulance before I kill you with a smile on my face motherfucker."

"Rodney this is Dr. Slade Buchanan." Angelina informed him quickly. "And I suggest you do what he says because he will definitely make good on his promise. Now shut the door and warn Lonnie not to open it. Have him talk to Sloan Murphy."

Rodney quickly shut the door, his face white as a sheet. Slade was heaving in anger as he glared at the door. His fangs had grown past his lips and Angelina knew he was on the edge of losing it and she had to pull him back to the present.

"There is a suture set on board." Angelina said trying to get Slade to focus on what was important, but she knew his worry for Jill was making him act irrational. She remembered doing an internship at University Hospital ER. The ER doctor she was shadowing was one of the best she had ever worked with until his father came in suffering a massive heart attack. Dr. Bradley Moore had fallen apart at the sight of his father dying in front of his eyes. That was exactly what was happening now. Jill had lost way too much blood and if it wasn't replenished, she would die. "I can start a blood draw on you, suture her up and then we can IV your blood to Jill. Do you think that will work?"

Slade was silent for a long minute then looked at Angelina. "It has to work." He responded and that's all she needed to hear. She stood to get everything set up, but he stopped her. "Thank you, Angelina."

She just nodded as she turned taking a deep calming breath. Please God, let this work, she prayed to herself.

She got the blood draw from Slade as he held pressure to Jill's neck, she grabbed the suture set. She then set up the IV so they could immediately start transferring Slade's blood to Jill. Glancing up at Slade who had been trying to get Jill to wake up she sighed. Jill not waking was not a good sign and they both knew it, but neither said it.

"Do you want me to do the sutures?" Angelina asked not wanting to overstep but had a feeling Slade's hands were not going to be as steady at hers in this moment. "I excelled in suturing."

That brought a small smile to Slade's face. "That is the one thing I didn't excel in, so yes, please."

Angelina nodded, then began as he removed the blood-soaked gauze. It wasn't easy in this cramped ambulance, but she made do. She worked quickly and efficiently. Slade worked in rhythm with her, wiping blood as she made ready to do the next suture. It was an ugly wound, but Angelina quickly, yet efficiently sutured it closed. Once it was done, she quickly cleaned up the mess, then started the IV. Slade sat back watching her every move as he held Jill's hand with his free one.

Once she was done Angelina grabbed more gauze then began to clean the wound checking her work. She also cleaned the blood off Jill's face gently until the only blood left was on Jill's clothing. "Can she get infection?" Angelina asked as she checked the drip of the blood in the IV.

"Yes, but my blood will wipe it out." Slade said staring at Jill's face. "I just don't know if this is enough blood. I don't want to give her too much of mine. Too much could make matters worse."

Angelina frowned also looking down at Jill. "When will we know?"

"She should have at least moved by now." Slade said, not even trying to hide the worry in his voice.

Looking up at the bag she felt true fear. Slade's blood was almost gone. "Can she take mine?" Angelina suggested. "I'm A positive."

"Type doesn't matter. We can conform to any type." Slade answered as he stared at her. "You would do that?"

Angelina frowned not liking that question. "Of course, I would do that. She's like a sister to me, Slade and I don't appreciate that question."

Slade sighed shaking his head. "Sorry. Not thinking clearly." Slade reluctantly let go of Jill's hand and stood.

Touching his arm, she stared up at him. "She is going to make it, Slade."

When Slade only nodded Angelina hurried to get everything ready for him to draw her blood. Once that was done, she sat down and rolled up her sleeve. Slade prepped her arm quickly. Angelina always hated the prick of the needle. It hurt like the dickens, but she sat there and took it. Her gaze went to Jill who lay silently as if she was taking a restful nap, but Angelina knew better.

"Her color looks better." Angelina mentioned, but Slade only mumbled as he focused on what he was doing.

After he was done Angelina rolled down her sleeve, then watched as Slade prepped Jill. If this didn't work Angelina didn't know what they would do. She moved so Slade could be close to Jill as she received her blood. Angelina moved as far back as she could, then slid to the floor and sat. Closing her eyes, she prayed like she had never prayed before that Jill was strong enough to pull out of this one. Her mind also went to the moment she saw Slade carrying someone out of the building. The fear she felt thinking it could be Adam had her stomach rolling again. Now that her mind was free to wander her stomach revolted. Grabbing a puke bag, she emptied her small breakfast into it. Closing it, she wiped her mouth knowing it was a one and done vomit.

"You okay?" Slade asked as he stared at her.

"Stress doesn't agree with me." Angelina said with a sigh. "Guess I'm in the wrong profession, huh."

Slade continued to stare at her for a long time. "No, you are absolutely in the right profession." Slade's tone was serious, as was his expression. "If you are ever in need of a job, consider yourself hired. What you have done today for Jill, I can never repay you."

"You owe me nothing, Slade." Angelina shook her head. "I would do anything for Jill."

"Does that include shutting the fuck up. My head is killing me." Jill's voice was weak and crackly, but it was her voice.

Slade jumped into action as Angelina breathed the biggest sigh of relief. Staring up at the ceiling she thanked the powers above for her answered prayers. Tears rolled down her cheeks as she slowly closed her eyes listening to Slade ask Jill medical questions and Jill snapping back, her voice growing stronger. A smile tilted her lips as the tears continued to fall. Her thoughts went directly to Adam and the rest of the Warriors. Their job was dangerous, she knew that, but today she learned just how quick they could lose one of them. How quick Adam could be totally lost to her. The fear of that thought overwhelmed her and sent Angelina straight to her feet. The urgency she felt to see Adam was undeniable and had her reaching for the side door.

CHAPTER 7

*J*ake handed the asshole he had in a headlock over to Damon. Sloan walked toward him with Steve following. "How is she?" Jake asked enraged that he wasn't able to stop the bastard from going after Jill in time.

Swallowing hard Steve shook his head. "It's not good, man."

"Fuck!" Jake cursed wanting to kill the son of a bitch Damon was taking away.

"Jill is tough." Sloan added, but there was a hint of worry in his voice. "Slade will pull her through."

He saw the wound that should have been healing but wasn't. That wasn't a good sign. Glancing down at the kids he saw Sid kneeling trying to calm them down. The older boy glanced his way and held his stare. He had to give the kid credit; he kept his shit during all of this. Even called the guy he was holding an asshole which had earned a grin and nod from Jake.

"Has the building been cleared?" Sloan asked, but Jake didn't answer because he wasn't the one clearing the building. That was Steve and Jill.

"Steve." Jake looked his way. "Did you and Jill finish clearing the building before you were attacked."

"Honestly guys, I don't fucking know." Steve replied looking not like himself at all and Jake knew it was because of Jill. He looked at Jake. "We were in here as long as you and Adam were outside."

Jake and Sloan shared a look. Before either could speak the older boy spoke up. "There was five of them."

"Five?" Jake frowned as his eyes gazed at the three dead laying on the floor.

"Yeah, five." The kid said with a nod. "Those three dead suckers and then the man that hurt that lady."

"You sure there was five?" Sid stood looking down at the kid.

"I can fucking count mister." The kid said with a deep frown.

"Hey, hey, hey...watch the mouth, kid." Sid said but was grinning.

"He's right, there was five of them." A younger girl said.

Jake's eyes went from the boy to the girl but landed on an even younger kid who was trembling. Their eyes met before she looked away and then up toward the ceiling, her little finger pointing upwards. Jake's eyes slowly followed her line of vision and saw the fifth bastard was posted in the corner of the ceiling watching every fucking thing going on.

Their eyes met just as he heard female voices. It all happened in mere seconds. Nicole walked in talking to Jessie who was right beside her and closest to the bastard, Adam followed. Before Jake could call out a warning, he knew the fucker was going to make his move. He had been spotted and was now trapped unless he found a shield to get him out. Jake made his move at the same time. There was no fucking way this asshole was going to use one of the women as a human shield, not on his fucking watch. Adam must have sensed something because just as he rushed that way Adam grabbed Nicole pulling her out of the way but missed Jessie.

Not wasting a second Jake grabbed Jessie around the waist swinging her out of the way of the vampire leaping from the ceiling, their feet tangled as he fell hard to the floor. Jake took the fall making sure she was protected, but the sight of the vampire lunging toward Jessie's back had him rolling so she was now on the bottom. Their eyes met for a brief second before hers shifted above him. Her mouth opened in warning, but he already knew and was ready.

With a quickness not seen by the human eye he shot his leg out catching the bastard in the chest sending him across the room, crashing through the wall. Sloan, Sid, Steve and Adam were already racing toward where the fucker disappeared. Turning he looked down at Jessie who was staring at him wide eyed.

"That was...impressive." She said, her voice breathless as she continued to stare at him.

"Are you hurt?" He asked looking her over as he sat up, then knelt. When she didn't answer he frowned staring into her beautiful light green eyes. Realizing he was staring he cursed, he repeated his question. "Jessie, are you hurt?"

"I don't think so." She finally answered as she sat up. "You took most of the fall. Thank you for that." Jessie actually laughed, then stood when he offered her his hand to help her up. She brushed off her jeans just as Nicole ran over.

"Well maybe Mitch was right." Nicole frowned looking Jessie over. "Maybe this job is too dangerous for you."

Jessie shrugged looking unconcerned. "And I could have gotten hit by a bus crossing the street this morning. Life is a risk. You either live it or you die wishing you had lived it."

"Good point." Nicole said with a snort.

"But how about we just keep this to ourselves. No need giving Uncle Mitch a heart attack." Jessie said, then started to follow Nicole, but stopped and looked up at Jake. "Thank you, Jake."

"You're welcome." Was all Jake could manage to say as he watched her walk away. Her long raven hair hung down her back swaying as she walked. With a curse he looked away and rubbed his eyes. What the hell was wrong with him. Guilt and a strong emotion of betrayal to Tracy hit him square in the chest.

"Been looking for you." Kane's voice broke him out of his thoughts. "And here I find you playing hero to a beautiful woman."

"Go away, Kane." Jake warned, his voice low. "I'm definitely not in the mood for your shit right now."

"Oh, really." Kane crossed his arms as he glared at him. "You know what I'm not in the fucking mood for? I'm not in the mood ever to hear my partner transferred from the Guardians to the Warriors without even talking to me first."

"I don't need your permission to do anything." Jake said already feeling guilty about Tracy, he sure as shit didn't need to have another guilt trip placed on him by Kane.

"A fucking heads up would have been nice, *brother*." Kane hissed back. "Not finding out from Charger who enjoyed watching me lose my shit."

Even though he and Kane weren't blood brothers, they were brothers in every other sense of the word. "Enjoyed it, did he?" Jake smirked then shook his head.

"Fuck yeah, he enjoyed it." Kane cursed then threw up his hands. "Why in the hell didn't you come and talk to me, Jake. If this is truly what you want then I'm happy for you, but if this is just you running from the past, I can tell you right now it's not going to work for long, if at all."

Jake had wondered more than once if this was him running from the past, and honestly, part of it was. Too many memories for him to handle and do his job well. There was a restlessness in his mind that he couldn't contain, and it was driving him crazy. He thought that maybe he needed a change of scenery and the only thing he could think of was transferring to the Warriors.

"It's nothing personal, Kane." Jake knew he deserved some type of explanation; he just wasn't sure he was ready to dive that deep into his own soul or at least what was left of it. "Just something I had to do."

"Yeah, well I'll let you slide this time fucker, but if you stop coming to poker night, I'm kicking your ass and taking your money." Kane said, then pointed at him as if driving his threat home.

"That's the only way you can take my money." Jake shot back, then grinned. "You suck at poker."

"Fuck you." Kane said flipping him off.

"You guys finished?" Sloan frowned glaring at them. "We could use some help over here, but of course, if you're still in the middle of your conversation don't let us bother you."

"Was that sarcasm?" Kane asked as he and Jake headed toward Sloan.

"If you have to ask you're a dumb fuck." Sloan responded, then turned to face them, but looked at Jake. "I need you to help transport the kids with Nicole. I've got Viktor and Bishop heading out with you."

"Where is the fucker?" Jake nodded toward the hole in the wall he sent him through.

Just then Sid and Damon were leading him out, their eyes connected and the asshole grinned as he was passing with a Warrior on each side of him. "Almost got you." His grinned widened showing his gleaming fangs. "And that bitch would have been mine."

Without thinking Jake's fist shot out landing on the bastard's mouth. He laughed and spat out blood, his eyes then turned deadly as did the sinister smirk that replaced the grin.

"I will see you again." He spat blood at Jake's feet, then looked back up into Jake's burning glare.

"Looking forward to it." Jake smirked back wanting nothing more than to end the fucker right now.

"You will be sorry for messing with the wrong people, boy." He continued looking back over his shoulder and he spat the words. "And tell that pretty lady I'll also be seeing her very soon."

Jake started to go after him, but Kane put a hand on his chest stopping him. "Let them get their information then we will find him." Kane whispered, then looked at Jake with a wink. "Just like old fucking times, brother."

Nodding, Jake watched Kane take off after Sid and Damon, running his mouth to the asshole they were escorting and had just threatened not only him, but Jessie. Yeah, he would definitely take Kane up on that hunt because he'd be damned if he would take the fuckers threat lightly.

Turning Jake stopped when his gaze met Jessie's. She was standing close and had to of heard what the bastard said, but there was no fear in her eyes. She walked up to him and leaned close. "Please tell me you'll take care of that before he does." She leaned away from him to stare up at him again.

To say he was shocked by what she just said would be a total understatement. Finding his words he then leaned close to her because the kids were very close. "Consider it done."

A slow smile of relief formed across her lips making her green eyes sparkle. The total acceptance of his promise surprised him. She then nodded, grabbing one of the little girls' hands and then proceeded to have all the kids form a train by holding each other's hands.

"Okay here we go you all." Jessie said as she began to move. "Remember not to let go of your partners hand."

Jake stepped back as the train of kids started to pass him. The little girl who had pointed out the bad guy on the ceiling looked up at him with a shy smile. He winked down at her as if they had a big secret.

"I'm too old for this shit." The older boy who had done all the talking rounded out the end of the train.

Jake fell in step as he followed them out, focused on any danger around them. The older boy kept bitching which was entertaining to Jake. He remembered when he was that age about a hundred or so years ago. As they climbed the steps his eyes rose to see Jessie looking back to make sure the children were all still abiding by the hand holding rule. Their eyes met again as she smiled at him, then turned and continued out of the building. The guilt once again rained down on him and he felt like total shit. This strange attraction to someone shouldn't be happening. He didn't understand it and it pissed him off.

"Dammit." Jake cursed himself as he climbed the last few steps.

"I know how you feel." The older kid in front of him snorted.

Jake grinned shaking his head. Fucking kid was a riot. Once outside he spotted the ambulance with most of the Warriors standing around it as if guarding the area. His eyes met those of Steve who turned to watch them exit the building. With a sad shake of his head Steve turned back around, Jake sighed. What a fucked-up reality they were all living in.

CHAPTER 8

Angelina opened the side door of the ambulance and stepped down. The brutal cold air hit her square in the face taking her breath away. The wind whipped her hair around as her gaze scanned the area. The Warriors stood around the ambulance, silent as if they were statues. Their eyes met hers as she slowly walked toward the back, her gaze searching for the one Warrior she wanted to see more than anything. She was a fool, she knew, but right now she just didn't care.

Just as she rounded to the back side of the ambulance her arm was yanked turning her toward a pissed off Rodney. "Who in the fuck do you think you are?" He hissed in her face. Hearing the growls around her she decided right then and there to save his stupid ass life.

As she started to push him away, he disappeared when Adam slammed him to the ground. "She is my fucking Mate you son of a bitch. That's who she is and if you ever lay a hand on her again or talk to her in that way, I will kill you. Do you understand me?"

To say she was upset seeing Rodney laying on his back staring up at Adam in fear would be a total lie. The guy was an asshole know it all who seemed to hate women who knew more than him. He was condescending even while he showed her the back of the ambulance as if she was a child.

Steve walked over and picked up Rodney. "I think he understands but guess we should make sure." Steve said looking at Rodney. "Nod three times if you understand that if you ever, and I mean ever, touch or talk to her like you did…you will die a very slow, excruciating death."

Rodney nodded three times without looking Angelina's way.

"Now get the fuck out of here." Steve gave him a shove, then looked at Angelina. "How is she?"

Angelina looked around at all the Warriors staring at her waiting for her response. "She is talking, but it's still early. She's lost a lot of blood."

"I want her fired." Rodney's voice grated on her nerves so bad which was sad. She just met him hours ago and she already wanted to smack him.

"Great. First day on the job and I'm fired already." Angelina sighed then stepped around Adam to confront the shitstorm that had become her life. "Lonnie I'm sorry, but—"

"Sorry ain't going to cut it when you hijack my damn ambulance." Rodney cut her off rudely. He then glanced at Adam who took a step forward, but once again she cut Adam off.

"It's not your ambulance asshole, it belongs to the taxpayers." Angelina informed him, then turned her attention back to Lonnie. "I'm sorry, but there was a serious injury, and I was assisting Dr. Slade Buchanan who is still working on the patient."

"Who by the way threatened my life." Rodney added pointing to the back of the ambulance.

"Shocker." Steve snorted loudly.

"I just may press charges." Rodney continued puffing out his chest, but his stomach protruded beyond that, and it just made him look ridiculous.

"You are going to clean up every speck of blood that *vampire* shed in my ambulance. And you will replace every single thing you used on it." Rodney snarled at Angelina. "I demand respect—"

Angelina's hand flew out and slapped Rodney across the face with a loud slap. After watching the life slipping away from her best friend to hear someone so disrespectfully call her a vampire with such disdain and then follow it up with calling Jill an *it* was all Angelina could take. Not feeling satisfied with just one slap she went in for another one, but Adam grabbed her around the waist and pulled her away.

"Whoa, killer." Adam said keeping an eye on Rodney to make sure he wasn't going to retaliate.

"You have no right to call her anything but her name. Press charges on me, asshole." Angelina yelled trying to get past Adam who was watching her wide-eyed. "And as for respect...you're a fucking EMT. If anyone deserves respect, it's me since I outrank your sorry ass. I wouldn't trust you taking care of a hot turd. Watching you today with that worried mother was pathetic. You want to talk about respect... you showed none to your patients. None! Piece of shit."

Angelina felt like she was going to hyperventilate. Never in her life had she ever let loose like that and holy hell it felt really fucking good not taking the high road for once. The Warriors around her began to clap and whistle as she tried to calm her breathing.

"Slow and easy." Adam whispered as he massaged her shoulder. "Slow and easy."

She began breathing deeply in through her nose and out through her mouth. She could still hear Rodney running his mouth but couldn't make out what he was saying because of the ringing in her ears.

Suddenly the back of the ambulance flew open as Slade stepped down glaring at Rodney. Angelina moved that way peeking in to see Jill lying flat, not moving.

"Oh, no." Angelina cried out as she started to get into the back, but Jill moved her head looking at her. The relief she felt sent her legs into wet noodle mode.

"Was that you doing all that cussing out there?" Jill's voice was weak, but Angelina heard her just fine.

"Maybe." Angelina said her face flushing. Jill was always trying to get her to cuss, but Angelina had never really been a fan of using that kind of vocabulary. That may have changed because cussing Rodney out felt...freeing.

"I knew I'd rub off on you one day. It's a proud moment." Jill chuckled then coughed, but held up her hand when Angelina

65

started to climb into the back. "I'm fine, thanks to you. Slade told me what you did. Thank you."

"Just doing my job, which I'm about to be fired for." Angelina said, then shrugged. "But it was worth it seeing your smiling face."

"You won't get fired." Jill assured her, then her eyes tried to go to Slade. "Just don't let him kill anyone. He's a little on edge."

"Are you the boss?" Slade was asking Lonnie as Angelina focused on what was going on.

"It doesn't matter. She is getting fired and sued." Rodney said not knowing when to shut up. "She hijacked my ambulance."

"This guy's an idiot." Steve muttered getting agreement from all the Warriors around him.

"If you say one more word, I will permanently shut you up." Slade warned Rodney before turning his attention back to Lonnie.

"Was that another threat?" Rodney said just as Slade punched out and doing as promised shutting Rodney up. He dropped like a sack of potatoes.

"Obviously not." Slade fired back even though Rodney was beyond hearing. He then returned his attention back to Lonnie. "I'm Dr. Slade Buchanan and if you fire Angelina Pride it will be the biggest mistake you ever make. She saved my Mate from certain death with her fast thinking while I couldn't form a thought because of my worry. She also gave blood to help replenish my Mates blood along with mine. Even under the stress of that so called EMT pounding on the door trying to evict not only myself and Angelina, but my Mate who needed immediate medical care which she got."

Angelina felt all eyes shift to hers, even Adams, but she continued to watch Lonnie and Slade. She was always uncomfortable with a lot of attention. She'd rather be on the outside where she was most comfortable looking in.

"I would however fire him because if that doesn't happen, I will speak personally to Sloan Murphy, and we will use another ambulance service if needed." Slade continued standing over Lonnie who was listening intently.

"Already have one in mind." Sloan who stood on the sidelines listening added.

"I'm truly sorry that happened. Though we do have certain protocols in place for new hires who we haven't received test scores yet, but this situation deems a little different than most." Lonnie said not looking nervous at all with all the Warriors glaring at him.

"Fuck the test scores." Someone in the crowd said and Angelina thought it was Jared's voice.

"Oh, I agree." Lonnie said to the crowd. "Rodney had the top score until…"

Angelina frowned when he looked her way.

"Angelina." Lonnie grinned at her confused frown. "Your test scores came in after you and Rodney left. I figured I'd tell you after your ride along. So, what happened today wasn't against any rules and even if it was, I'd look the other way. People save lives, not test scores."

"And what about him?" Slade motioned toward the now snoring Rodney.

"Oh, he's definitely fired." Lonnie said without hesitation. "He's already had complaints, but honestly we are so short staffed it's difficult to let anyone go. But yes, he will be informed of his termination as soon as he wakes up."

Slade turned to look at Angelina then nodded before climbing back into the ambulance with Jill. Lonnie stepped over Rodney and headed toward her.

"Well, that was…" Lonnie tried to think of a word to describe what just happened.

"Scary." She added with a slight smile trying to help him.

"Yes." He nodded then laughed wiping at his brow even though it was freezing. "Good job, today. And I'm sorry I paired you with Rodney, but I figured if you could handle him then you could handle a lot of dicey situations."

"Yeah, he definitely is one of a kind." She replied glancing over at Steve who was using his boot trying to rouse him.

Angelina felt Adam close behind her, the warmth of his body radiating throughout hers. She wanted nothing more than to lean back against him to soak it up, but didn't. Nothing had really changed and for her to do something like that just wouldn't be fair to either of them, yet she wanted to so badly.

"I need to get Jill to the hospital." Slade stuck his head out looking first at Lonnie and then to Angelia. "Can you drive this thing."

Angelina looked toward Lonnie who was watching her. "Well, can you?" Lonnie asked with raised eyebrows.

"Yeah, I can drive." Angelina replied, then frowned. "Is she okay?"

"No, I'm not." Jill called out from the back of the ambulance. "So go fast with the lights on."

Angelina looked at Sloan for confirmation on that and when he grinned shaking his head then chuckled. Total opposite of the man she had seen only minutes prior. "She's better, but I want to get a blood count on her. She may need more."

"I've got plenty." Angelina offered without hesitation.

"No, we've taken enough of yours." Slade responded then went back inside closing the door.

"You sure?" Lonnie watched her closely. "I can take them."

"Have to learn some time." Angelina said, then laughed. "Joking. One thing Rodney did right was show me repeatedly where everything was and what it was for, even the gas pedal and brake. I got it."

Lonnie rolled his eyes. "I'll send the next shift to pick up the ambulance at the hospital and take you home."

"That won't be necessary." Adam finally spoke. "I'll see her home."

Lonnie nodded, then stuck out his hand toward Adam. "Nice to meet you, Adam. And one hell of a football game."

Adam shook his hand and smiled. "Thanks."

Lonnie walked away then began trying to wake up Rodney, Angelina looked up at Adam. "I can get an Uber."

"You've got to be spending a fortune on Ubers." Adam teased but when she didn't smile, he sighed. "We need to talk, Angelina."

Never had she been able to say no to Adam Pride and dammit she didn't want to start now. Or did she? Her head nodded as her heart screamed no. Maybe it was time that they talked, actually he was going to be the one who did the talking because she had said everything she needed to say already.

Walking around him she opened the back of the ambulance. "Got the patient strapped in?"

"I do." Slade affirmed with a nod.

"Lights and sirens." Jill lifted her head looking at her. She still looked pale and her eyes were glassy, but she was sounding more like the Jill she loved.

"If this isn't an emergency situation I'm not breaking the law, Jill." Angelina informed her as she shut the door.

"Dammit, I need to work on her a little bit more. Finally got her cussing like a sailor, now I have to get her living a little more on the edge." Jill was saying as she closed the door.

Angelina chuckled as she turned to see every Warrior behind her. She stopped confused on what they were doing. Sloan walked in front of them and slammed his hand on his chest. The rest of them followed. Her eyes met Kent's then went back to Sloan's in confusion before looking at Adam who was doing the same, but the pride in his eyes shined brightest and it made her feel...special again.

"Thank you for saving one of our own." Sloan's deep voice filled the parking lot. "It will never be forgotten."

"She's worth saving." Angelina said as her tears filled her eyes, but she forced them to stay hidden. "She's as much my sister as she's yours. I'd give my life for her."

"You did." Steve walked up giving her a tight squeezing hug. "By giving her your blood. Thank you. I don't know what we would do without Jill."

And so it went each Warrior quickly approached her showing her their appreciation for taking care of one of them and it truly meant the world to her. Adam walked up to her last and pulled her into a tight hug.

"Thank you. I've always been proud of you, Angelina. That may not mean anything to you now, but just know there is nothing in this world that compares to you in my eyes or in my heart. I love you and always will." He whispered, then let her go and walked toward his bike.

Angelina turned just as the tears fell. She glanced up to see Slade watching her out the back windows. She quickly wiped her eyes. He gave her a nod before disappearing. Hurrying to the ambulance she checked to make sure Rodney hadn't taken the keys, but surprisingly they were in the ignition. Starting the ambulance, she let it run for a minute as she wiped her eyes clear of tears. With a huge deep breath, she put it in drive and took off.

"What a way to start out a new job and career." She said, then laughed shaking her head. "Only you, Angelina. Only you." She repeated something her mother always said to her. Glancing in the side mirror she saw Adam riding slightly behind them and sighed. This definitely wasn't how she thought this day would turn out, but so far it had been a doozy and didn't seem to be letting up. As long as she kept the guard around her heart secure, she should be okay. She glanced once again in the mirror at the red light, her eyes met Adam's golden ones and she felt the guard slip slightly and it absolutely terrified her.

CHAPTER 9

*A*dam stood just outside the room that Jill was taken too, Angelina was inside with Jill and Slade. One of the EMT's had come in to inform Angelina that they were taking the ambulance, but Adam assured them that he would let her know and that she did in fact have a way home. Adam frowned at the word home. She wasn't home until she was under the same roof as him. He just hoped he hadn't fucked that up.

"How's she doing?" Steve took him out of his thoughts as he and Jake with Dillon taking up the rear walked toward him.

"She's okay." Adam replied with a nod to Dillon. "She needed more blood, but Slade said she should be good to go soon. She's still not healing quickly, so the sutures Angelina applied on the wound will have to stay."

"Ah, shit." Steve snorted. "She's going to be walking around like some badass."

"Having your throat practically ripped out kinda makes one a badass." Jake said with conviction. "She earned that title in my book."

"I swear to hell and back." Steve grumbled. "One day I am going to have that title."

"What title?" Charger asked as he and Raven walked up to the group. "Dumbass? I think you already have it."

Adam grinned at that cocking his eyebrow waiting for Steve's reply which was sure to come.

"No, badass." Steve frowned at what he just said. "I mean you're not a badass..."

Charger's eyes narrowed at Steve.

"I mean you are a badass, but that's not what I meant." Steve tried to explain himself but was failing miserably. "I want the title of badass. Jake said Jill earned that title because she got her throat ripped out."

"I'll rip your throat out." Charger said, then shrugged. "If that title means that much to you."

"Why do I even open my mouth?" Steve leaned against the wall with a huff.

"I wonder that every day." Adam smirked then laughed at the look Steve threw his way.

"Dude if that was me laying in there, you'd be pacing the hallways worried to fucking death about me. So don't act like you wouldn't be shedding puddles of tears at my demise." Steve informed him in the most serious tone.

"Puddles?" Dillon cocked his eyebrow at Steve.

"Yes, of tears." Steve said then did the happy fingers toward his eyes. "Rivers just flowing out of his eyeballs."

"You're seriously fucked up." Raven laughed at Steve's antics as Adam rolled his eyes.

"Where in the fuck were you today?" Adam asked hoping to stop Steve's bullshit.

"Sloan had me chasing my ass in Dayton." Dillon said not looking happy about the fact.

"He transferring you?" Adam frowned hoping that wasn't the case. He liked having Dillon around. Reminded him of the old days as they had grown up together.

"I hope the fuck not." Dillon said with a curse. "I'll quit before I get transferred again. I missed home."

Soon the hallway was filled with Mates and Warriors. A few of the Guardians showed up also. It was always like that when one of their own was down. The support for each other even when tempers soared was always there. It was one thing Adam enjoyed most because he and Tessa hadn't grown up with this kind of support. Thoughts of his father wormed its way into his mind, but he shoved them away. Now definitely wasn't the time.

"Any word?" Sloan showed up with Becky at his side. It was strange seeing the big bad Sloan holding hands with his Mate. Adam didn't know why, but it was just weird. Sloan could rip your fucking heart out before you even knew what was happening with the hand he was gently holding Becky's with. Yeah, strange.

"She required more blood, but she is improving quickly. The healing process is slow, so they are keeping the sutures in place." Adam said loud enough for those who came in later and he didn't have to repeat it again.

"Damn." Sloan cursed with a frown. "I don't like hearing that about her healing slow. What about you? Have you been healing slow? Dillon?"

"Not human slow, but not as quick as you pure bloods." Dillon replied first.

"Same." Adam replied knowing why Sloan asked just them. They had all three been given the same serum that turned them.

"Why in the fuck is it different for her?" Sloan asked, but didn't expect an answer, but Steve was ready to supply one.

"Probably because she's a female. They are slower at every-thing compared to a male." Steve said absently not realizing how close to death he just became.

"Excuse me?" Raven's head snapped toward him as all the women glared at Steve.

"I said...oh." Steve started to repeat until he realized what he said and who he said it in front of.

"I know what the hell you said." Raven growled taking a step toward Steve. "What I don't know is if you believe the bullshit that just came out of your mouth."

Steve snorted opened his mouth, then shut it again. Looked at Adam for help, but Adam just stared at him as if he had lost his fucking mind.

"Leave the kid alone." Jake grinned at Raven. "He just says shit to say shit. Isn't that right Steve?"

"Exactly." Steve said as he pointed at Jake. "I say shit to say shit. I've said it before and I'll say it again to save my ass... I'm a big shit talker. Half the time it just falls out of my mouth and I'm like oops, what just fell out of my mouth...it's shit."

"Are you fucking finished?" Sloan asked with a warning that he better be fucking finished.

"Shutting the fuck up." Steve said before Sloan could say it.

Steve squeezed himself between Jake and Adam against the wall. "Do you ever listen to yourself?" Adam asked glancing at Steve.

"Obviously I need to work on that." Steve whispered since he just told Sloan he was shutting the fuck up.

"Adam, I need to talk to you." Sloan said then whispered something to Becky before he headed down the hallway away from everyone.

"Thank fuck he said you and not me." Steve whispered giving Adam an encouraging nod. "I've got your back, friend. Whatever it is I have you...back here against the fucking wall."

"Steve shut the hell up." Adam glared at Steve as he passed. As he headed down the hallway to where Sloan went, he saw Daniel give Sloan a nod as he passed.

Sloan took a seat in an empty waiting area up the hallway. Adam took a seat opposite of him wondering what the hell was going on. He had just said something to Dillon about transferring and if Sloan was going to want him to transfer Adam would have to refuse. There was no other reason he could think of that Sloan would single him out to talk to him. He had already given his full account of what happened today.

"Listen, Adam. I'm not good with this shit." Sloan said, his gaze serious as he stared at Adam. "I know you've been having some personal issues. I don't know much, but I know enough."

"Sloan whatever is happening in my personal life is not affecting my work. What happened today was no ones' fault." Adam jumped the gun to defend not only himself, but Jill, Steve, and Jake.

"I'm not talking about today." Sloan leaned back in the chair crossing his arms over his chest. "What happened today could happen to any of us at any time. I place blame on no one other than the bastard who thought it was a good idea to fuck with the Warriors."

"Then what is this about?" Adam frowned knowing that he did his job and did it well.

"I just want you to know that if you need anyone to talk to my door is open." Sloan said in a serious tone. "And if you need time off put in for it and I'll make sure arrangements are made so you can take care of your business."

To say he was shocked would be a total understatement. He remained silent as they stared at each other. Finally, he found his voice. "I appreciate that Sloan." Adam said and meant it. For Sloan Murphy to take even a second out of his busy life to make time for him and his issues meant a lot. "I'm working on my personal stuff, and I promise it won't affect my work."

Sloan actually laughed. "Son, anytime there is trouble with our Mates it not only affects our work, but our whole fucking life. Just know my door is always open."

"Thank you." Adam said with a small grin. He then hesitated as he thought for a quick second to voice his feelings, but then changed his mind. He really needed to figure this out on his own. Standing Adam cleared his throat. "And yeah, Mates can turn our worlds upside down."

"So can killing your father even if they are a bastard." Sloan also stood as he threw that bomb out in the open. Adam's eyes snapped to his, but he remained closed lipped. "I should know. I killed my own piece of shit father. To say it didn't fuck me up for a minute would be a lie, but I didn't let it change me or ruin my life. He needed to die."

"Why?" Adam said then realized what he just asked. "Sorry, you don't have to tell me. Though you know exactly why I killed mine."

"It doesn't bother me to talk about it. I let him stop controlling me a very long time ago. He ruined not only my life, but my brothers and sister as well as my mothers'. I was the oldest of four brothers and one sister. He was an abusive piece of shit. I planned it all and once I was big enough, I saw the deed done and have no regrets whatsoever. I didn't then and I don't now." Sloan said, his eyes narrowing slightly. "He had never laid a hand on my sister until one day I saw him dragging her to the woodshed with his belt. That was the day he died. My mother ended up hating me for it, but she was never beaten again after that."

"You weren't changed then?" Adam asked another question, but he couldn't help himself.

"I was human." Sloan answered, then clapped Adam on the back. "I know you well and I know that you would never kill anyone, especially your own father, if it didn't need to be done. Stop letting him control you because that is exactly what he is doing from the grave. You are nothing like your father, if you were you wouldn't be working for me. I know you and Tessa had a rough life growing up, but that's over. Don't live in the past and don't let your past dictate your future. Angelina is a special girl, Adam. If you let what happened with your father ruin what you've done with your life to this point, then you should have just let him live."

Sloan's words were like a punch to the gut because they rang true. "How did you know?" Adam finally said as they walked out of the small waiting room.

"I know all, Adam." Sloan said then chuckled just as Daniel made eye contact with them both and Adam knew the truth. "You have a lot of people who care about you and Angelina. Sometimes it takes seeing through someone else's eyes that you're fucking up one of the best things in your life."

Just then his eyes caught Angelina walking out of the Jill's room, the Mates swarmed her giving her hugs. Her gaze scanned the area and he could only hope she was searching for him when they found him the relief he saw had him realizing that maybe he wasn't too late and hadn't fucked up too bad. There was still a chance for them.

"Make it right." Sloan said as he walked away heading toward Becky.

"Yes, sir." Adam said as he stopped and waited for Angelina to be free. Steve walked up and behind him staring at him. "What in the fuck are you doing?"

"Seeing if your ass was still there." Steve said, with a grin. "It's still there. What in the hell was that all about?"

Adam glared at Steve then laughed. Damn, this guy. He just had one of the hardest talks with Sloan and now he was laughing at Steve's dumbass. He just ignored Steve's question as he waited for Angelina anxious to get out of there so they could have a much needed and long-awaited talk that could possibly change his life forever.

CHAPTER 10

"Get out of here." Jill said as she sat on the edge of the bed. "I'm fine and don't need you hovering over me."

"I'm not hovering." Angelina rolled her eyes as she sat in the chair watching Slade take more blood. She knew that was exactly why Jill was being moody. She hated needles and pain. Though Angelina would not complain about listening to Jill complain. They had come very close to losing her.

"Dammit, Slade." Jill jumped as Slade put the needle into her skin. "You're taking all the blood you just gave me. I'm fine and just want to leave."

"I'll tell you when you're fine." Slade informed her. "Hold still."

Jill rolled her eyes with a huff. "I'm a bad patient."

"Yes, you are." Both Angelina and Slade said at the same time.

Angelina laughed as she stood up once Slade was finished. "You sure you don't need me to stay?"

"No, I'm good now." Jill reached out and hugged her tight. "Thank you, Angelina. For everything. Slade told me everything when you were driving us here."

"I was just doing what I know how to do." Angelina played it off as nothing. "Just promise me to be more careful next time. I really don't want to see you like that again."

"Deal." Jill said giving her one more hug.

Angelina headed for the door as Slade was giving the nurse Jill's blood and giving her directions. Once the nurse left, he grabbed Angelina in a hug before letting her go.

"Remember you will always have a job with me if things don't work out." Slade reminded her then turned back toward Jill. She watched as he gently touched Jill's cheek as he checked her wound. He whispered something to her as Jill reached up to touch his cheek. She turned quickly and walked out the door only to be swarmed by all the Mates. Her gaze scanned the area looking for Adam as she answered questions.

She was anxious to see him and hear what he had to say. She couldn't stop thinking about him saying they needed to talk. Was she finally going to get answers to what happened? Did she really want to know? Her stomach clinched at that thought and then her heart thumped loudly as her gaze landed on his. Adam was walking up the hallway with Sloan as Steve approached him then started looking at his ass.

Adam looked mad at first until Steve said something which transformed Adam's face into the Adam she missed so much. He then looked her way, his smile slipped slightly as he stared at her and she wondered if it was her that changed him into the stranger he had become. That thought made her sick to the point she wanted to throw up.

"Good job today." Kent said as she was finally free from the questions.

"Thanks, Kent." Angelina said giving him a smile.

Butch and King also gave her an approving nod as they all three headed down the hallway. She saw them stop to talk to Adam and didn't know what to do. Should she go to him or just wait for him to approach her. God, she hated this. When things were good she would rush to him. Now she didn't know what she was supposed to do. Did he change his mind? Did he still want to talk? Feeling lonely in a hallway full of people had her sinking into herself. Something she did when she felt out of place. Walking toward the wall she decided she would wait for him to come to her. She refused to put herself in a position where she could be hurt.

Slade walked out telling the Mates they could go in and see Jill. Raven walked past, but stopped. "Solid thing you did today, Angelina."

"Just did my job." Angelina repeated what she had been saying because it was true. That was her job, even though it was totally different doing it on someone she cared so much about.

"You ever need anything don't hesitate to give me a call." Raven said as a sinister smile curved her lips. "I can even straighten Adam's ass out. I can take him easy."

Angelina laughed. "I will definitely keep that in mind."

Raven gave her a wink before walking into Jill's room. It was good to know badass people Angelina thought with another chuckle. She sure as hell was happy that Raven was on her side.

"You ready?" Adam's voice made her jump.

"Yeah." Angelina nodded, but then frowned. "Don't you want to see Jill first?"

Adam glanced toward the room where all the Mates were crowded into and shook his head. "Yeah, I think I'll wait on that. I'll text her later. She's fine though, right?"

"She's going to be fine." Angelina nodded as they started the walk toward the elevator. Nerves hit her hard making her feel like they were on a first date or something. It was strange. He pushed the elevator button, and it opened immediately as if waiting for them. They stepped inside and then rode down to the first floor in silence.

They walked out as the elevator opened heading toward the exit. The snow was coming down at a heavy clip. Adam took his jacket off and started to help her put it on, but she stopped him. "I'm fine Adam."

"It's cold Angelina and it doesn't affect me. You on the other hand will freeze on the back of my bike." Adam didn't take no for an answer. "You look good in your uniform he said after putting the jacket on."

"It's grey." Angelina frowned down at her paramedic uniform. Lonnie already had it ready for her knowing that she would be working there. "No one looks good in grey."

"No one does, but you definitely rock it." Adam said with a grin and wink.

Angelina slowed as they walked toward his bike. Usually his wink would win her over no matter what, but tonight it did the opposite. It was a warning to her heart.

"What's wrong?" Adam frowned as she came to a complete stop.

"I can't do this?" Angelina whispered doing her best not to cry. "I really can't. If you think your grin and wink is going to make me cave, then I have to guard myself Adam. Just one wink from you can make me forget everything and I can't do that to myself, not anymore. I'm sorry."

She turned to start walking away, then realized she had his jacket on still. She started to take it off, but he was there turning her around to face him. "Just hear me out. That's all I ask, Angelina. I promise I won't grin, wink, touch, or anything, but please hear me out."

The conflict between her head and heart was brutal as she stood there watching the snow fall between them. Finally, she nodded. "Okay."

"Thank you." Adam said and even sighed in relief.

"Bev is away visiting family for the holidays. We can go there." She informed him as they made their way across the slick parking lot. After she slipped once he held her elbow to keep her steady. Finally, they made it to his bike. He got on first, started it and then she slipped on. Riding with him was one of her most favorite things in the world to do. She missed it so much. Not many people would ride in the snow, but the Warriors were a different breed. Angelina trusted Adam to get her from point A to point B even in the snow.

He made her put a helmet on which was fine because honestly it was freezing out and would keep her head warm. As he took off, she wished she had a pair of gloves because her hands became instantly numb. Adam must have known because at the stop light he lifted his shirt and placed her hands on his bare skin then covered them with his shirt.

"Just to keep your hands from freezing." He said over the roar of the bike wanting to make sure she knew he was not trying anything funny and dammit that made her love him even more.

All the way to her apartment she tried to prepare herself for what was to come. She really didn't have any idea what was going to happen, but she was more than willing to hear him out as he called it. All she knew at this moment is what she would accept from him and if it wasn't him in this marriage a hundred percent with her then she would file for divorce. She deserved no less and she would accept no less. If she was putting a hundred percent so would her partner and that was something she would not compromise on...ever.

CHAPTER 11

*J*ake walked toward the white marble tombstone. Reaching out he touched it as he did every time he visited. At least two inches of snow lay on top, and he noticed little impressions across the snow. Tracy's favorite bird was the red bird and every time he visited one was always here, or one showed up before he left. No matter what time of day or night. He never left here without seeing one except for the last time he visited, and it had bothered him, still did. Seeing the tiny impressions in the snow made him feel somewhat better.

Hearing the crunch of snow behind him he knew exactly who it was. "You can stop trying to be sneaky. I know you're there."

"I'm not being sneaky." Raven said from behind him.

"Obviously since you sound like a heard of elephants." Jake said then grinned as he turned to look at her over his shoulder.

"Yeah, well fuck you, Jake." Raven said, then grinned. "Asshole."

"How you doing, Raven?" Jake asked as he turned back toward the tombstone.

"Oh, you know living the dream." Raven replied as she walked up and stood next to him also staring at the tombstone. "Heard congrats was in order. Decided to switch sides did ya?"

"Felt it was time for a change of scenery." Jake replied then glanced her way. "What no gloating?"

"Who me? Gloat?" Raven said with a fake surprised look on her face. "Never."

"Can I ask you a question?" Jake said after a few minutes of silence.

"Shoot." Raven replied looking his way.

"Have you seen any red birds lately when you come here?" Jake asked as he looked at her.

Raven frowned as she thought about it. "Actually, no I haven't, but it is winter so maybe they went south."

Jake knew that wasn't true because he had seen plenty of them in other places, just not here. He had thought that was Tracy sending him a message that she was still here, but now he wasn't sure. He knew that sounded crazy, but it had comforted him many times since Tracy's death.

"Can I ask you a question?" Raven asked after they were once again silent for a long minute.

"Shoot." Jake repeated what she had said to him.

"Was Tracy your true Mate?" Raven asked the question point blank, no punches pulled.

"Why would you ask me that?" Jake felt his body tense but forced himself to relax. "I loved Tracy, Raven."

"There are a few reasons I asked you that." Raven stated then added. "And I have never questioned your love for Tracy."

"What the fuck are your reasons?" Jake growled not liking this conversation, but for some crazy reason he couldn't walk away from it.

"If I lost my Mate and had a chance to talk to him from the grave I would jump at that chance. Why haven't you talked to Lana or Caroline when they specifically want to give you a message from your Mate?" Raven turned to full on face him.

"And your other reasons." Jake didn't look at her just kept staring at Tracy's tombstone and the tiny impressions.

"If I lost my Mate, I would not be looking at another man the way you look at Jessie." Raven said without hesitation. "Especially this soon after losing my Mate."

Jake sighed then shook his head. "Nothing in my fucked-up life affected me more than Tracy's death. I wanted to kill myself, Raven and if it hadn't been for Kane I probably would have. I loved her more than my own life."

"Again, I am not questioning your love for her. I saw it, lived it with you guys, but that doesn't mean you were Mates." Raven kept pushing and it was starting to piss him off. "I know it's none of my business."

"You're right it's not." Jake knew those words wouldn't stop Raven, but he still had to voice them. "What the fuck does any of this matter now? She's dead."

Raven pulled something out of her jacket and laid it on top of the tombstone and the tiny impressions. "It matters because you deserve the happiness, and you know Tracy would want that for you as well. All I see is you living through the guilt of not being able to save her."

"What is that?" Jake's eyes narrowed at the small journal like notebook.

"Chantel packed some of her stuff and sent it to me. Chantel told me that Tracy gave her instructions that if anything happened to her who got what. We all know how anal Tracy was with her things." Raven replied then added. "And to answer your questions…that is the truth. Ever since I've known Tracy, she kept a journal about everything."

Jake stared at the journal for a long minute before he responded. "If you think you know the truth then why the questions?"

"Because I want to know why?" Raven stated then reached out and touched his arm. "And because I want to see you happy, Jake. I think Tracy would want the same thing. I'll leave the journal for you, but please think about talking to Lana and Caroline. They've been patient, but I know Tracy has been persistent with them and they will eventually come to you themselves."

Jake didn't respond just stared straight ahead. Raven finally turned and started to walk away, but stopped. "I love you like a brother Jake and I'm not doing this because I want to. I feel that I have to do this for you as well as Tracy. I don't know why, but it's just a feeling. If you don't make the decision to talk to Lana and Caroline, then I'm going to. I just don't want to do it because I'm not sure how that works. If it's a one and done deal or what. If that's the case then the one chance to talk to Tracy is yours, not mine."

Hearing Raven walk away Jake waited until he was sure she was gone. He then fell to his knees as he slowly reached out running his finger over her name. He then pressed his palm against the stone as his head fell forward.

"I'm so sorry, Tracy. It should have been me, not you." Jake whispered; his voice rough with emotion. "I will always love you no matter what."

Lifting his head his eyes rose to see a red bird standing on the journal Raven left. It tilted its head staring down at him. All he could do was remain still and watch as it hopped off the journal, then back on it over and over again. Standing slowly, he reached out and took the journal not taking his eyes off the red bird. It tilted its head once more before it took off leaving him alone.

Looking down at the journal he backed up and sat in the snow as he leaned against the tree. Jake didn't know how long he sat there just staring at Tracy's handwriting on the front of the journal trying to decide if he wanted to read it or not. He had always had his suspicions but had loved Tracy enough to never question things that seemed not quite right.

Opening the journal his eyes scanned the pages without really reading anything. He knew he would find all the answers but couldn't bring himself to discover them yet. Jake shut the book with a curse.

Raven was right. There was something about Jessie that pulled him to her. He had never felt it before, not even with Tracy and that was hard to admit. The guilt he felt was overwhelming that he just shoved those feelings away. He'd rather live alone for the rest of his life instead of betraying what he thought he had with Tracy.

Closing his eyes, he leaned his head back against the tree trying to bring the vision of Tracy's face, but every fucking time he tried since meeting Jessie it was her face he saw. "Fuck!" Jake growled in frustration.

Knowing he had to know the truth he opened the journal randomly then looked at the date. Their wedding day. Once again, he looked away having a hard time bringing himself to read what Raven called the truth.

Forcing himself to read the first line told him that his suspicions had been warranted. It was for sure in Tracy's handwriting.

Today is the day I marry the man I love and betrayed...

Jake slammed the journal closed. He finally had the truth from Tracy herself. He didn't need to know any more than that. Standing he walked over and put the journal back on the headstone, then walked away not noticing the red bird had come back to stand on the journal as if guarding it.

CHAPTER 12

$\mathcal{A}$dam followed Angelina into the apartment closing and locking the door behind him. He scanned the apartment, his gaze falling on a folded blanket and pillow on the couch. Adam frowned knowing that small couch was where Angelina slept. She didn't deserve this, dammit. What in the fuck had he done to them. Sloan's words kept coming back to him, had opened his eyes to how selfish he had been.

"I'm going to change really quick." Angelina broke into his thoughts.

Nodding Adam watched as she walked to the corner of the room where clothes were neatly piled. She knelt sorting through things before standing up and heading to a door before disappearing. Walking over he looked down at the clothes, her clothes that lay on the floor in neat piles. She didn't even have any place to put her things. He had done this to her. Hating himself even more at that moment he cursed, turned away and walked toward the only window. He stared out at the snow-covered street. It was coming down hard and fast, the wind blew the white flakes sideways.

"Sorry, but I had to get that uniform off." Angelina's voice had him turning around. His eyes soaked her in. She wore a huge hoodie that swallowed her frame, sweats, and fuzzy socks. She had piled her hair into a messy bun looking more beautiful than he had ever seen her.

"I'm sorry." Fell from his lips and for a split second he thought of fucking Steve who had dumb shit falling out of his mouth daily. Yes, Adam was sorry, sorrier than he had ever been in his entire life, he could say it and yet, she deserved much more than a fucking, I'm sorry. The disappointed look on her face told him she also knew she deserved much more than that.

"Adam, if that's all you came here to say you can leave now. I've got to get up early for my first official shift tomorrow and I still have to clean blood stains out of my uniform." Angelina walked to the door, unlocked, and opened it. "If you need clarification from me to move on, fine. I accept your apology. Now please leave. I'm tired, so very tired."

He could see the tears she was fighting to keep at bay, and it killed him inside. He was doing this too her, continued to do it to her and it was going to stop. Walking over he closed the door, locked it then took her hand and led her to the couch.

"I killed my father." Adam stated as he sat beside her but continued to look out the window and not at her.

"I know that, Adam." Angelina replied, her voice held that softness that drew him in. It was a comfort to him to hear her talk. Growing up all he heard was yells, bellows and a harshness that stayed with a kid through adulthood. "I don't like to say this because I'm in the business of saving people, but he deserved exactly what he got. Do you know how many times I've wanted to off my stepfather? Still do at times especially when I see my mother with a fresh black eye."

"He's hitting her again?" Adam frowned hearing this. That son of a bitch had been warned multiple times. A visit was in order it seemed.

"Yeah, I had breakfast with her. She was wearing those huge sunglasses I hate." Angelina snorted with a shake of her head. "So see Adam, you are not the only person in the world who—"

"Killed their father?" Adam snapped then wished he hadn't. Reigning in his anger, not at her, but himself she sighed. "Sorry."

"That's not what I was going to say, but it's a moot point." Angelina said not seeming to take offense to him snapping at her. "You had no choice, Adam."

"I'm terrified that I can't be the man that you deserve, Angelina." Adam stated the one true fear he held close to his chest. "When I look in the mirror, I see him in me. There are things I do that mimic him and I absolutely despise myself when I do them. How can I even be the man you deserve when deep in my soul I hate myself."

Adam finally turned to look at Angelina and what he saw in her gaze had him shooting to his feet.

"Do not fucking pity me." Adam tried to keep his voice to a low rumble, but the rage he felt inside him was part of his father and when it came out of him, he couldn't control it, just like that bastard couldn't control it.

Adam was surprised when Angelina shot to her feet, grabbed his arm, and turned him to face her. There was no pity in her eyes now, just deep anger that was directed at him.

"Pity is one thing I don't feel for you, Adam Pride." Angelina's voice raised. "But anger sure as hell is. You are nothing like your father. Would you ever raise a hand to me?"

"You know the answer to that." Adam shot back not even liking the insinuation that he would.

"That's right I do know the answer to that." Angelina held his arm tight in her grip so he couldn't turn away from her. "I know a lot of answers that concern you and do you know why I know those answers? Let me tell you, because I have loved you for a very long time. I loved you when you walked past me not even acknowledging my existence."

"Dammit, Angelina." Adam snarled glaring at her. "I know I treated you badly, but in my defense I didn't know how you felt about me. That is history and doesn't have anything to do with anything other than rub salt in my wound or is that what you want? Payback for the way I've treated you in the past and present."

The slap was fast and hard. "Fuck you." Angelina growled, then slapped him again. "And fuck you again."

This was not how he saw this conversation going. No matter what was just said he couldn't help but like this new side to Angelina. Holy shit his face was burning like fire.

"If rubbing salt in your wounds will wake you up then I'll buy all the salt in the world to do just that." Angelina was far from done. "Do you honestly think I could love someone like your father?"

"My mother did." He responded quickly and spoke the truth. Rose Pride loved their father more than anything, but she also feared him.

"I am not talking about your mother, Adam." Angelina said, her voice calming somewhat. "I'm talking about me. Do you think I could ever love someone like your father. My home was a revolving door of men who treated my mother like dirt. I grew up with some of the worst sleeping in the room next to mine and every night I heard my mother crying because of physical or emotional abuse, or because they left her. Every single night as a child and teenager I swore to myself I would not follow in her footsteps. I would not fall for one of those men like my mother brought home. And to this day I never have."

Adam's anger cooled somewhat as he really listened to what Angelina was saying. He searched her eyes and knew she spoke the truth.

"The first time I saw you I feel in love, deep crazy love that scared me to death. I followed your every move like a stalker stalks its prey. I spent every minute I could learning every-thing about you that I could because I had to know what kind of person held my heart because of the promise I made to myself." Angelina's voice was that soft comforting tone again. "I never missed a football game, I went to parties alone just so I could watch you with other people and all I saw was kind-ness, Adam. Everyone loved you and not because of you being the star quarterback. They loved you because you were a decent human being. And when you finally did notice me, you were kind to the nerdy quiet girl that no one paid attention to. That Adam, is who you really are."

The silence hung between them as they stared at each other. Neither moved for a minute as they both absorbed what had just been said. Adam had come here to talk, but Angelina was the one doing all the talking and what she was saying held truth he couldn't deny. Didn't want to deny because that meant he wasn't the monster he was afraid he was slowly turning in to.

"Your father was evil, Adam." Angelina reached out and touched his face then pulled it away. "You are not only a VC Warrior whose main purpose is to rid the world of evil, you are also a man who has high morals and because of that it had to be you who killed your father. As hard as that may be to hear, it's what I believe in my heart, and I always listen to my heart. That's why I never gave up on us."

Adam felt a tear escape his eye as he stared down at her. It shocked him because he was programed not to shed a tear. Had been slapped and humiliated as a small child for even looking like he was going to cry. 'Men don't cry you little momma's boy.' His father's voice rang in his head. Even hearing his father's voice from the grave still trying to humiliate him, he refused to wipe the tears that were now flowing freely.

Angelina walked into his arms and held him tight as he digested everything he needed to hear but had refused to listen.

"I know you better than anyone in this world, Adam Pride." Angelina whispered against his chest. "I think it's time that you learn yourself exactly who you really are because you've been wrong for a long time. You are not your father and never will you be your father."

Adam squeezed her tighter, but then realized it may be too hard and loosening his arms slightly. He could feel her tears soaking through his shirt, but he didn't care. "It was never about you, Angelina. Please believe me when I say that. It was never about anything you did."

"I know that now." Angelina said as she pulled away to look up at him. "But Adam you have to open yourself up to me and if not me, then someone. Carrying the world on your shoulders all the time is the path to destruction of everything in your life."

"I love you. I've missed you so much. Let's get you some things together and get out of here and go back to our apartment." Adam whispered as his lips carefully touched hers. She kissed him back briefly then laid her head on his chest, but he had felt her stiffen. Adam frowned realizing she didn't say 'she loved him' back. Slowly he pulled her away from him to look into her eyes and what he saw terrified him. Had he been too late?

CHAPTER 13

*A*ngelina stared into Adam's eyes as he stared down at her. Her heart felt somewhat lighter, but she knew that they just scratched the surface of their problems.

"Angelina?" Adam's voice was deep with emotion. "I said I love you."

'And I love you, Adam." Angelina hesitated slightly before she answered. "I never stopped, and I will always love you."

"You're not leaving with me, are you?" Adam felt her loss as she moved away.

"No, I'm not." Angelina said then added. "Not yet anyway. I think it's important that you work this out on your own, Adam. I know you heard the words I spoke, but those were my words, not yours. Until you truly believe you are not your father, I can't put myself back in that situation to be ignored again, set aside…no matter what the reasons are."

Adam rubbed his face in frustration. "I did that because I was afraid you would see me for the man I thought I was becoming."

"I did see you as the man you were becoming." Angelina smiled sadly. "We just saw two different men. Adam, we will be fine. I just think it's important you focus on yourself without having to worry about upsetting me. That is what is important now."

"Bullshit." Adam finally said then grabbed her coat and helped her put it on.

"What are you doing?" Angelina struggled getting her coat on over her hoodie. She watched as Adam grabbed her boots, then took her arm leading her to the couch. She sat down as he put her boots on for her. "Where are we going?"

"For a ride." Adam said as he helped her up then zipped her coat.

"But it's freezing out there and looks like a blizzard." Angelina argued not knowing what in the hell was happening as he grabbed her hand, led her out the door then locked it. He then picked her up and carried her through the snow to his bike.

After they were both on, he took off sliding in the snow. Angelina trusted Adam fully when it came to his riding skills, so she wasn't worried about safety. She did however wonder where in the hell they were going. The snow was beautiful as it floated in the streetlights that they passed so she decided to trust him and enjoy the frigid ride.

Adam turned off the main road which looked like a path between some tall pine trees. It could have been a road or driveway, but with the snow cover it was hard to tell. Looking over his shoulder she spotted a farmhouse in the distance. The closer they got the more familiar it became.

"Oh, my God." Angelina gasped as Adam came to a stop. It was the farmhouse she saw in one of the home seller ad papers she looked through constantly. She had seen it on the pages and fell in love instantly. She had told Adam that was the one she wanted. He had frowned said it was too old and too expensive, but Angelina never lost hope. Even put it on her project board hoping to manifest it one day.

Adam helped her off the bike since her mouth was still wide open as she stared at the house. The conversation she had with her mother about Adam buying her a home came to her, but she remained silent not wanting to spoil this moment, if in fact, it was a moment. She wasn't totally sure what kind of moment this was...their house moment or they were trespassing moment.

"I went out the next day after you showed me this house and bought it. I've been working on it every free chance I've had." Adam said proudly, but there was a sadness to his voice. "I don't want you sleeping on someone's couch anymore or having your clothes on the floor. I've been staying here to work on it when I'm alone because I can't stay at the apartment without you. It's just too hard without you there. This is your home, Angelina."

Tears were freezing on her face as she stared at the house and hearing the pride in Adam's voice had her jumping into his arms. "It's our home, Adam." She kissed him then turned to look at it again. "Can we go inside?"

Adam chuckled as he picked her up and carried her to the porch, keyed in a code at the door and walked inside. "Duncan put in the security for me. I've only done structure work because I want you to pick out everything else. The colors, appliances, flooring and whatever else this old place needs. There is also ten acres that belong to us. So whatever animal you have your heart set on we can get. They already have a pretty decent chicken coop."

"Animals? I can have animals?" Angelina was still in Adam's arms as she looked around, her eyes missing nothing.

"Anything you want, Angelina." Adam said looking down at her. "Susan I'm sure will give you plenty of pointers on chickens and a garden when spring gets here."

Walking further into the house Adam showed her each room, then stopped at one of the three bedrooms. "This I figured could be our room." He set her down and she walked further into the bedroom. She went to the window that looked over the front yard. Slowly she closed her eyes as her excitement dimmed.

"What's wrong, Angelina?" Adam walked up behind her obviously feeling her mood shift.

How could she answer that when she wasn't sure herself. The memory of her mother always forgiving the men who treated her like shit because they bought her a ring or some kind of worthless piece of jewelry clouded her mind. Was she looking at this house the same way? Was this her piece of jewelry?

She let Adam turn her around, his hand cupped her chin bringing her face to his. "I am sorry for what I've done to you, but I promise you that every single minute I have free will be spent here with you working towards our future. I fucked up,

Angelina. If you just give me a second chance I promise to never let you down again. It's a promise I will die to keep. I will work on my daddy issues." He gave her a half grin at that. "And I will be open with you about my feelings. You are my wife, my Mate and belong here with me building our future."

Angelina heard every single word and truly believed him, but there was one thing she needed to make absolutely clear. "I have one promise I want from you, the most important because if you achieve that then everything else will fall into place."

"Anything Angelina. For you I will promise anything." Adam said with such sincerity Angelina wanted to cry.

"You have to work on your...'daddy issues'...for you and only you. Not for me. Not for Tessa. For you. No matter what happens between us you must do that for yourself." Angelina searched his eyes watching for his reaction to her demand and yes, it was a demand. "If you can't do that then I need to walk out of here now."

Adam stared at her for a long time before speaking. "You love me that much?"

"Yes, Adam, I do and have forever." Angelina replied without hesitation.

Stepping back Adam slammed his hand to his chest as he bowed his head and knelt to his one knee. "I swear to you Angelina Pride that I will work every day on my issues with my father so that I can live the life that was meant for me, and that life involves anything and everything that has to do with you. This I swear as not only a VC Warrior, but as a man."

Tears flowed down Angelina's face as she watched Adam vow his promise to her by way of a VC Warrior. Not many would understand the magnitude of that vow, but she did and knew Adam did not make it lightly. Neither did she.

Adam stood slowly, his eyes searching hers. "Was that enough of a promise?"

Angelina smiled reaching up wrapping her hands around his neck. "Can we get my things tomorrow. I don't want to leave tonight."

"Really?" Adam's smile grew wide.

"Really." She nodded as she held him close and knew she was where she needed to be, in his arms and in their home. She knew there was work to be done on their relationship, but she had to trust her heart and her heart told her that Adam was ready to face his demons. Her heart also told her not to let him do it alone.

The kiss started slow then grew to a full blown make out session. Before things went too far Angelina pulled away. She tried to speak but had to stop and catch her breath. "I want to see the property."

"Now?" Adam frowned trying to reach for her, but she danced out of his reach.

"Yes, now." Angelina actually played the big football player when she faked him out and passed him running out of the room and down the steps. She screamed as she heard him pounding down the steps behind her, but kept going toward the front door. Amazingly she made it outside and into the snow. Bending she scooped up a handful and formed a ball, turned and let loose hitting Adam square in the chest.

"Oh, you are going to pay for that." Adam growled as he scooped up his own handful of snow.

Angelina took off laughing and weaving hoping not to get hit. She tried to scoop as she ran, but slid and fell. Before she could get up Adam was on top of her keeping his weight off her with his arms on both sides of her. The smile he wore faded as he stared down at her.

"You are so beautiful." He whispered as he lifted one hand to brush snow off her face. "My very own snow angel."

Feeling a tear slip from her eyes she saw the love for her in his gaze. She knew at that moment she wasn't making a mistake. This man loved her, never stopped loving her.

"Adam." She whispered his name.

"Hmmm." He leaned down and kissed her softly.

"Take me home." Angelina sighed finally feeling a peace.

He stood then bent and picked her up without a word. Turning he walked back toward their home, their future. Angelina kept her gaze forward vowing to never look back again.

CHAPTER 14

$\mathcal{A}$ ngelina was rushing around excitedly while Adam was pulling pizzas out of the oven. "Hurry, everyone is going to be here any minute."

"Hey, Sid is coming and if I burn these damn pizzas, I will never hear the end of it." Adam grumbled with a serious expression.

Angelina chuckled as she watched him. It had been a month since she first walked into this home, well since Adam carried her and it had been a very busy month. The house was almost complete, and she was in absolute love with it. Tonight everyone was coming to see their new home and she was so excited she could just burst.

She and Adam had also been working on their relationship during the remodeling. Adam at times fell into that dark mood, but always came to her instead of staying absent. They would end up doing a small project together or just go walk the property and talk. Sometimes they talked about his feelings or struggles, sometimes about hers or they just walked in silence. The key was they did it together.

Angelina always remembered something her mother had told her. Sometimes our worst struggles end up being our best successes. She had to admit as hard as it had been for her to walk away from Adam, she truly believed if she hadn't, they would still be in the same pattern they had been in, and would eventually end up hating each other. Not that Angelina could ever hate Adam. Her love for him was too deep. Maybe a strong dislike. That thought made her grin.

"What are you grinning about." Adam wrapped his arms around her resting his chin on her head.

"I'm just happy." Angelina smiled snuggling against him.

"We might have time for me to make you a little more happy." Adam teased as he cupped her ass giving it a soft squeeze.

"Are you ever satisfied?" Angelina gave him a fake frown then squealed when he picked her up and sat her on the counter.

"Oh, I'm always satisfied when I have you, but I'm a selfish bastard and want more." He kissed her neck then laughed. "You remember when you slapped me…twice."

"Yes." Angelina frowned, but the grin won out. "You totally deserved both of them."

"It turned me on." Adam admitted with a wiggle of his eyebrows. "I like you, hot and bothered. Maybe later you can give me a few slaps."

"I was not hot and bothered." Angelina shot back. "I was angry and pissed."

"I'll have to see what I can do about that later. Maybe piss you off a little." He continued to nibble on her neck, and she had to admit it wouldn't take much for her to allow him to take her right there on the counter."

Suddenly there was a loud knock on the door. Adam cursed; Angelina squealed. "They're here!" She tried to hop off the counter, but Adam blocked her. "Adam someone is at the door."

"Yeah, well they are going to have to wait." Adam said just as Angelina's eyes fell to the bulge in his pants.

Deciding to play dirty since he made her horny as hell she licked her lips as she looked up at him. "Too bad we got company." She cupped him and gave him a squeeze. "I have something for that." As he pushed into her hand she pulled away and moved past him toward the door.

"You'll pay for that later." Adam warned her with a growl.

"Looking forward to it." She shot back just as he disappeared. Opening the door she smiled as Steve, Mira and Drew stood at the door. "Come in."

"I knew we were going to be the first ones here, but Mr. On Time had to leave a half an hour early." Mira rolled her eyes as she gave Angelina a hug.

"You guys could have come earlier than this." Angelina smiled as she picked up Drew who was growing like a weed. "You are always welcome here."

"Where is Adam?" Steve looked around with a frown. "Can't he welcome his guest?"

"He, ah, will be right here." Angelina tried not to giggle knowing exactly what Adam was doing and actually felt a little jealous that she wasn't in there helping him out. Her body tingled at the thought. Lately they just couldn't get enough of each other. It was a miracle the house got done at all. "How about a piece of pizza that Uncle Adam made." She asked Drew who nodded eagerly.

"The house is beautiful, Angelina." Mira smiled as she looked around. "I'm so jealous."

"It was a lot of work, but it's been so much fun." Angelina said proudly. "I absolutely love it here."

Steve and Mira walked into the living area, Drew followed with her piece of pizza. "It's about time you got out here and welcomed your guests." Steve said as Adam walked in.

"You aren't guests." Adam teased, then winked at Mira.

"That was fast." Angelina snickered at his frown, then backed up as he stalked toward her.

"Not when I had plenty of visions in my head." He cupped her breast and squeezed knowing that Steve and Mira were busy with Drew in the other room. Just then there was another knock on the door. "Saved by the knock."

"You have no idea." Adam said with a wink, then went to answer the door.

Soon their home was filled with Mates and Warriors who were their family. Sid did bitch about the pizza, but Adam took it in good stride. She watched as Adam took Sloan aside. They were in a deep conversation, and she was shocked when Adam reached out and gave Sloan a hug that was given back. Her eyes met Steve's who was also watching then turned toward her and mouthed the words, 'Holy Fuck' then walked away wide eyed.

She had given everyone a tour, and now they were all enjoying each other's company in their home.

"What are you doing in here alone?" Adam walked up setting his drink on the counter.

"Just soaking in everything and thinking how very lucky I am." Angelina smiled up at him. "We did good didn't we Adam?"

"You did good by yanking a knot in my ass and those two slaps didn't hurt none either." He said with a grin and wink.

"Will you stop with the slapping nonsense." Angelina tried to sound serious but failed miserably. "And what in the world does yanking a knot in my ass mean?"

"Something Gramps used to say to us all the time when we were being bad. It sounded painful so we usually straightened up really quick." Adam laughed then grabbed her up for a quick kiss. "Come on, let's go mingle with our guests."

"I never thought I would hear the word mingle come out of your mouth." Angelina laughed shaking her head right before he kissed her. "You go ahead, and I'll be there in a minute."

"I love you." He winked then gave her a quick kiss.

"Love you more." She countered as he walked away. She watched Steve approach Adam.

"Dude did Sloan hug you?" Steve asked in awe. "Scared the fuck out of me. I thought the damn world was ending."

Adam laughed putting his arm around Steve as they joined the rest of the gang. "Not today, Steve. Not today."

~

*J*ake drove one of the SUVs through one of the neighborhoods he had been assigned. He had been invited to Adam and Angelina's, but declined making up some excuse so lame he couldn't even remember what excuse he used. He wasn't even scheduled to work today, but instead of doing nothing he was running his shift as if he were scheduled. He could have hung with Kane, but he didn't even want to do that. Kane saw too much and ever since talking to Raven and seeing Tracy's journal it was best he keep to himself for a while.

Seeing a familiar figure crossing the street in front of him he frowned. "What in the hell was she doing down in this area?" He said to himself as he was the only one in the vehicle. She slipped and almost fell in the slush on the road. Jake watched as she laughed at herself but kept on going. His eyes scanned the area for any signs of danger as he pulled off the road in front of the building she disappeared into.

His gaze scanned the building then went to the ground floor window when a light came on. Jessie walked past the window and disappeared. He waited for a few minutes not sure what to do. Should he go check to make sure she was okay? What the hell was she doing down here? Why in the fuck did he seem to care so much what she was doing? Hell he didn't even know her last name.

And then she reappeared and began to do…stretches. He then noticed a bar that ran the length of the room, or at least the window with mirrors running behind it. She grabbed onto the bar and began doing some weird moves. His eyes narrowed as he realized what he was watching. She was a dancer.

He sat memorized watching her like a stalker, but he didn't care. He was captivated by her, couldn't take his eyes away if he tried. Tracy was beautiful, but this woman was different and what he was feeling went soul deep. Finally he looked away realizing he was gripping the steering wheel so tight it was cracking.

"Fuck! What is happening?" Jake squeezed his eyes shut trying to figure out what in the fuck was going on. Glancing back he noticed people going into the building holding the hands of little girls with dancing costumes. He didn't know what the fuck they were called, but he had seen them before. His gaze went to Jessie again who was hugging each child that walked up to her. Her welcoming smile had him smiling as he watched.

Knowing he should leave; Jake couldn't make himself do it. He sat there watching for he didn't know how long. His eyes watching Jessie's every move. He felt like a fucking pervert watching her like he was, but he didn't care. It was innocent or was it. The feelings he was having right now sure as fuck didn't feel very innocent.

Jake laughed a few times watching the kids try something Jessie showed them. He noticed that Jessie never seemed frustrated with the children, but smiled and helped them until they got it. Even though he couldn't hear a word that was being said, he could tell that each word she spoke to the children was positive.

The kids sat down as Jessie disappeared for a second then reappeared. She stood in a position for a few seconds before she began to move her body in a dance that once again held him captivated. He could faintly hear the music coming from the building. The dance didn't last long, and Jake was disappointed when it ended. He watched all the children clapping. Jessie laughed just as her eyes rose and looked straight at him. Her smile faded slightly as she took a step toward the window then stopped. He saw fear flash through her eyes and wondered about it. Did he frighten her? He hadn't meant to, but then her grin widened as she recognized who he was. She lifted her hand and waved. Jake only nodded, then gave her a half grin before putting the car in gear and drove off glad it wasn't him that put the fear into her eyes. Now he was wondering what or who did put the fear there and swore he would soon find out, but first there was something he had to do.

Jake grabbed his phone and hit speed dial putting his phone on speaker.

"Yeah?" Sid answered and Jake could hear everyone talking.

"It's Jake." Jake said.

"I know. There's a thing called caller ID." Sid responded in his usual smartass manner.

"Tell Lana and Caroline I'm ready to talk." Jake said, then hung up before Sid could say anything else smartass.

It was time and before he could figure things out, he needed to hear from Tracy and if these sisters really could do what they say they could do it was his only choice. Turning around he wanted to drive past where Jessie was once more because it was a bad neighborhood. At least that was the lie he was telling himself.

Made in United States
Orlando, FL
20 May 2024